"Lara—go away, all right? It's over. We aren't a couple anymore, okay? I don't even know if we're friends."

She shook her head rapidly. "I don't believe it," she said. She stuck her hands out, as if she had suddenly lost her balance. Then she grinned at him. "Unless there's somebody else . . . "

Jake looked over Lara's shoulder. He could see Kate now, in her black miniskirt, dancing with her head down and her red hair flailing wildly over her shoulders to the monotonous, steady beat of the reggae band. Until he had seen her, he had thought he was going to tell Lara no.

"Yes," he said. "There is. Only she doesn't know it."

"I don't believe you, Jakie."

Jake looked her in the eye. "Believe it." He pushed her away, then lost himself in the crowd.

Don't miss any of the books in
Making Out
by Katherine Applegate
from Avon Flare

Coming Soon

Who loves Kate?

KATHERINE APPLEGATE

AN AVON FLARE BOOK

AVON BOOKS, INC.
1350 Avenue of the Americas
New York, New York 10019

Copyright © 1996 by Daniel Weiss Associates, Inc.,
and Katherine Applegate
Published by arrangement with Daniel Weiss Associates, Inc.
Library of Congress Catalog Card Number: 98-93670
ISBN: 0-380-80871-4
www.avonbooks.com/chathamisland

First Avon Flare Printing: August 1999

AVON FLARE TRADEMARK REG. U.S. PAT. OFF. AND IN OTHER COUNTRIES,
MARCA REGISTRADA, HECHO EN U.S.A.

Printed in the U.S.A.

WCD   10 9 8 7 6 5 4 3 2 1

Who loves Kate?

Zoey

How would I define friendship? I'm not sure, exactly. I do know, that whatever it is, it's important to me—especially these days. Spring break starts in a week, which means that graduation is right around the corner. In a matter of months, I'm going to have to say goodbye forever to the friends I've known all my life. It's scary.

But what's even scarier is that I'm less sure now than ever before of what the word "friendship" really means.

Until this past fall, I probably would have said that friendship means knowing and trusting somebody completely. There was a time when I thought I knew most of my friends as well as I knew myself. As far as I was concerned, we were one, big, happy family—and nothing bad or unexpected could happen to us as long as we stuck together.

I guess I was pretty naive.

I know now that it's impossible to know or trust someone completely. Even your own parents. This became clear to me when I happened to walk in on my mom and Jake's dad in the sack together.

Yet in spite of the cheating and the lies and the arguments my parents were able to salvage their marriage. Well, "salvage" is an understatement. They act like newlyweds. (It gets pretty gross sometimes.) So I guess a big part of friendship is also forgiveness—which is exactly what saved my relationship with Lucas.

But Lucas is more than just a

friend. After all, "friends" don't constantly pressure you to have sex with them. So what is "friendship"—pure and simple, without the complications of other things? As I said, I'm not really sure. No two friendships are alike.

Take my friendships with Nina and Jake. I relate to them in completely different ways—and not just because Jake is a boy (and not just any boy, either, but my ex-boyfriend).

Nina is my best friend. But in a lot of ways, we're opposites. I don't mean the obvious things: that she listens to horrible music, dresses like a member of Green Day, and smokes—yes, smokes—unlit Lucky Strikes. Nina can find humor in any situation. That's what I love about her the most.

On the other hand, my friendship with Jake is based

on his ability to take things seriously. We've helped each other get through so much that isn't humorous: his brother's death, our parents' affair—even our own break-up.

And then there's Aisha, and Claire...

I could go on. But I'd only be rambling. I've known most of my friends all my life, so maybe I've taken my friendships for granted in a way. The truth is that I don't have the slightest idea <u>what</u> friendship is.

One

"You have *got* to be kidding me," Aisha Gray said, frowning.

"Yeah, Zo," Nina Geiger added slowly. "I mean, no offense or anything—but this is by far one of the worst ideas you've ever had. It's almost as bad as wanting to throw a surprise party for Benjamin."

Zoey Passmore looked across the cafeteria table at the skeptical faces of her two friends. Her smile quickly faded. This was *not* the response she'd been anticipating.

"Come on—spring break in Miami," she repeated, as if the sound of the words would get them to change their minds.

Nina and Aisha exchanged glances.

"Well, *I* think it sounds amazing," Zoey said defensively. "We've never done anything like it. Besides—it's going to be one of the last chances we ever have to do something as a group."

Nina poked listlessly at the lukewarm spaghetti on her plate. "Uh—I don't think I need to remind you of this, but the last time we did something 'as a group,' somebody almost got their skull fractured."

Zoey sighed. Nina was referring to Benjamin's surprise birthday party, last Friday night. And she was right—Zoey *didn't* need to be reminded of it. In terms of the many huge disasters that had occurred in her life so far, the party ranked up there with the worst of them.

Ever since the operation to restore his sight had failed, Benjamin had been floundering in a severe depression. It was frightening. Zoey had never seen anything like it—not even since Benjamin had gone blind almost eight years ago.

He no longer had a sense of humor. His grades were failing. He stayed home from school more often than he went. And worst of all, he lashed out violently at those who were closest to him. His behavior had changed so drastically that he even claimed he wanted to break up with Nina—although Zoey was certain that couldn't last very long.

So Zoey had thought that a surprise birthday party would be just the thing to cheer him up—to show Benjamin that everyone loved him and supported him. From the start, nothing went right. First, Benjamin demanded to know why Lara wasn't there. Then Aaron Mendel had promptly arrived, unannounced and uninvited. After making a general jerk of himself (no huge surprise), he picked a fight with Lucas. Lucas lunged for him—and ended up accidentally punching out his new houseguest (and Aaron's former fling), Kate Levin. Benjamin's surprise birthday party ended in the waiting room of Weymouth General Hospital. The only saving grace was that Kate had suffered no permanent damage.

After that fiasco, Zoey was in no hurry to throw any more parties. But what she had in mind now was different. *Very* different. It was a change of pace—a way to get off the Island and to get away from their parents, a way to just let loose and have a good time.

"Come on, you guys," Zoey pleaded. "You have to admit it sounds fun."

Before either of them could reply, Claire Geiger strolled up to the table and put her tray down. She tossed her long black hair aside and glanced around the table suspiciously. "What sounds fun?" she asked.

Zoey swallowed. "I . . . uh . . . ," she stammered.

"Zoey wants us all to go to Miami for spring break," Nina said dully. "She's finally gone over the deep end. Hence the crazy fantasies and the speech impediment."

"Miami?" Claire smirked. "Gee, Zoey. Your imagination never ceases to amaze me."

Uh-oh. This was precisely what she wanted to avoid. She knew the older Geiger sister would be less than thrilled unless she felt she would be gaining something concrete from the trip. Zoey had been hoping to get Aisha and Nina to agree to it first. Three-on-one was a lot easier than one-on-one.

"Look—I admit, throwing a surprise party for Benjamin probably wasn't the greatest idea in the world," Zoey said. "But this is completely different. I mean, like I was just telling these guys, we've never done anything like it before."

"Probably for a reason," Claire muttered under her breath. She twirled her spaghetti on a fork and looked at Zoey thoughtfully. "How would we get there? Flights aren't exactly cheap."

"We'd drive. We'd take my parents' van. I talked to them about it this morning." Zoey paused. "Hopefully we could take somebody else's car, too."

Claire raised her eyebrows. "I wonder whose car that would be. . . ."

"Hey, Zoey—have you talked to Benjamin about this?" Nina suddenly asked.

"Not yet," Zoey admitted. In fact, the more she talked about the trip, the more she began to think that maybe the whole thing *was* a stupid idea. For the past two days, her vision of cruising down the highway to a sunny, tropical, beachside paradise had been the only thing keeping her from losing her mind completely. In theory, it sounded great. But now she was beginning to wonder if Nina was right. Maybe she *had* gone over the deep end.

Claire lifted the fork to her lips, then hesitated. "I bet I could convince my dad to let us use the car," she said nonchalantly.

"*What?*" Nina cried.

Claire took a delicate bite and shrugged. "You know, as crazy as it sounds, I don't think it's such a bad idea. I could use some time away from Chatham Island myself. Who knows? Maybe we'll actually have some fun for a change."

Zoey's eyes widened, but she kept silent. A little grin formed on her lips. Without a doubt, Claire had some secret motivation behind her decision. She always did. But Zoey wasn't about to let that stop Claire from influencing Aisha and Nina.

"So who else would be coming?" Claire asked.

"Well, Benjamin and Lucas and Jake, obviously," Zoey said.

Claire smiled coldly. "Obviously."

"Uh—am I hearing things right here?" Nina asked. "Are you two really serious?"

Claire blinked. "What's the problem, Nina?"

"Oh, no problem," Nina said. "I'm really psyched to cram into a car with my *ex*-boyfriend for thirty hours. And I'm looking forward to all the fun-filled activities Florida has to offer, like getting skin cancer and staying at some cockroach-ridden motel. Sounds perfect."

Claire rolled her eyes. "I didn't know you were so worried about your complexion, Nina."

"Look," Zoey said hastily, "we're not gonna stay at

8

a cockroach-ridden motel. And as for Benjamin, I think he *needs* a little change. I mean, don't you think a little distance and perspective—and time alone with his friends—will make him realize how stupid he's been acting?''

Nina didn't respond.

''You know, Nina,'' Aisha said in a tentative voice, ''Zoey may have a point.''

''Yeah,'' Claire added. ''After all, road trips have worked wonders for you guys in the past. . . .''

''That was the past,'' Nina snapped, glowering at her sister.

A strained silence fell over the table. Zoey knew very well what Claire was talking about. So did everyone else. She was talking about the time Nina and Benjamin had secretly gone to Boston. Nina ended up losing her virginity on that trip. It was still weird for Zoey to think about her best friend and her own brother having sex— but it wasn't nearly as disturbing as another memory that flashed through Zoey's mind, unbidden and un- wanted. It was the memory of Claire and Benjamin kiss- ing in Benjamin's room, not four nights ago. What on earth could have prompted Benjamin to kiss Claire—or vice versa? Their relationship had died long ago. Zoey shook her head. It was best not to think about it. Nina was right: that was the past. They needed to focus on the future.

''What's wrong, Zoey?'' Claire asked.

''Huh? Oh, nothing.'' She leaned forward and put her hands on the table. ''Look, you guys—I'm not taking no for an answer. This trip is gonna happen.''

Aisha ran a hand through her long, brown curls. ''I really don't know,'' she said doubtfully. ''I was plan- ning on using the break to study.''

''Wait a sec, here,'' Nina said. ''I thought you already *took* the exam for the Westinghouse prize, or whatever it's called.''

''I did.'' Aisha lowered her eyes. ''But I still have a bunch of papers, and there are exams at the end of the semester. . . .''

''Eesh—there's something all of us have been meaning to tell you,'' Nina announced with exaggerated earnestness. ''You have a problem. You're a full-fledged nerd. But there's hope, and we're here to help you. . . .''

''Ha, ha,'' Aisha replied flatly.

''Seriously, Eesh,'' Zoey said. ''Nina's right. If you think about it, this semester doesn't even really *matter*.'' She glanced conspiratorially at Claire. ''I mean, college applications are already in. There's nothing we can do at this point. So . . .''

''So we might as well party,'' Claire finished for her. She dropped her fork and put her face in her hands. ''Oh, no. I can't believe I just said that. I sound like a sorority girl from southern California.''

''Besides, if anyone should be worried about school, it's me,'' Nina interjected. ''I'm the only one here who still has another year.''

Aisha frowned. ''What are you saying, Nina?''

''I'm saying that I'm willing to sacrifice my own illustrious academic career as long as it means keeping *you* from studying.''

Zoey tried to contain the wide, silly smile breaking on her face. *Two down and one to go*, she thought. *Come on, Eesh. If anyone always caves in at the last moment, it's you.*

Aisha gave Nina a blank stare. ''Even if it means spending a week with your *ex*-boyfriend?''

Nina waved her hand dismissively. ''We'll ride down in separate cars. Besides, Miami is crawling with cute guys. I know they're all just dying to meet an exotic

10

beauty like me. Maybe I'll even be picked for one of those MTV contests. You know, those ones where you have to lip-sync the words to *As Long As You Love Me* in a bikini? And then you get judged by twelve gorgeous muscle-bound studs with a collective IQ of thirty-four?''

Aisha stared at Nina. Finally she started cracking up.

"So does this mean you're in?" Zoey asked.

"Fine, fine," Aisha mumbled. "I'm in."

Lucas Cabral stood in the middle of the cafeteria floor, clinging to his tray and feeling like an utter fool. He stared through a few wisps of long, unruly blond hair at the table where Zoey and the rest of the Chatham Island girls were sitting. They were all laughing hysterically. He shook his head to get the hair out of his face. Why were they so giddy? It didn't make any sense. Hadn't they all endured one of the worst weekends of their lives?

He scanned the room for a place to sit. Finally he spotted Jake, alone at the opposite end of the room. He hesitated. There was a time, not so long ago, when the idea of sitting with Jake McRoyan would have seemed completely absurd—if not downright dangerous. After all, Jake had once made it painfully clear that he intended to make Lucas's life a living hell. Not that Lucas could blame him. Lucas *had* spent two years locked away in Youth Authority for killing Jake's brother, Wade. And then, of course, Lucas had stolen Zoey away from Jake almost the moment he'd been released. . . .

But lots had changed in six short months. Once Jake had discovered Lucas was innocent of killing Wade, he no longer insisted that Lucas be treated as an outcast. And recently—after the two of them had spent a long, thoroughly miserable evening with Lara McAvoy

11

(which had included, among other things, cleaning Lara's vomit off Jake's bathroom floor)—they had even managed to flesh out the beginnings of an awkward peace. It was pretty amazing, actually.

Lucas sighed and headed toward Jake's table. As he threaded his way through the crowded cafeteria, he cast one last glance at Zoey. He always resented the way the Island girls excluded the Island boys from their lunches. It wasn't that he wanted to sit with Claire or Nina or Eesh, necessarily. But why would Zoey want to sit with *them* when she could sit with her own boyfriend instead?

Because girls need "girl talk," he said to himself resignedly. *A hell of a lot more than guys need "guy talk."*

He slouched down at the table across from Jake. "What's up, man?" he asked.

Jake looked up and nodded. "Not much." His face was expressionless.

Lucas dug into the greasy spaghetti on his plate. Jake wasn't exactly a big conversationalist—but that was cool. Lucas could easily enjoy his lunch in silence.

"Hey, uh, how's that girl who's staying with you?" Jake asked. "What's her name . . . Kate?"

Lucas managed a grin. "Oh, her. You mean the one I nearly killed."

"Yeah." Jake laughed shortly. "That one."

He took a deep breath. "She's fine. She has a little bruise on her face, but that's about it. We all rode to the hospital in the ambulance with her." He shook his head, still reeling from the memory. He felt sick every time he thought about it. The way she had just collapsed to the floor, blood gushing from her nose . . . it was too much.

"Man, I still can't believe I did that," he said out

12

loud. "But she was really, really cool about it."

Jake nodded. He had an odd, preoccupied look on his face. "I'm—ah—glad she's okay." He returned to shoveling spaghetti into his mouth.

Lucas looked at him for a moment. "Hey—what happened to you that night? You just kinda disappeared."

Jake shrugged. "I didn't feel like sticking around," he said with his mouth half full.

"Yeah, I can understand that. Neither did I."

Jake's eyes flickered. "Who invited Aaron, anyway?"

Lucas felt his muscles tense at the mention of Aaron's name. "Nobody. He crashed."

Lucas still couldn't *believe* that jerk would show up at the Passmores' after all the grief he'd caused. Aaron should have been banned from Chatham Island permanently a long time ago. Lucas couldn't remember ever hating anybody so much. It wasn't even that Aaron had fooled around with Zoey behind Lucas's back; Lucas had gotten over that. It was far more that he was a lying, cheating, stuck-up, pretty-boy snob who thought he could get away with anything. He had been a jerk to every single girl he knew—Zoey and Kate and Claire and probably dozens of others. What could they possibly see in him?

". . . poor Benjamin," Jake was mumbling. "What a way to spend your twentieth birthday."

Lucas wrenched his thoughts back to the table. "No kidding," he said glumly. "He didn't come to school today. Again."

"That kid's gotta snap out of it." Jake slurped up the last of his lunch and let his fork clatter to the plate. "I'm starting to get worried about him. Seriously."

Lucas nodded. "I know what you mean. The whole thing is starting to bum Zoey out in a major way."

13

"Nina, too," Jake muttered. "That girl's been acting like even more of a freak than usual." He stood and gathered his tray. "Oh, well. Catch you later, man."

"Later." Lucas watched as Jake took the long way out of the cafeteria in order to avoid passing the girls' table. He couldn't help but smile. He and Jake had a lot more in common than Jake probably realized. Aside from the obvious—that they'd both been involved with Claire and Zoey—they probably both felt pretty much the same way toward Nina and Aisha as well.

Nina is a basket case, and Aisha . . . well, she's nice enough, but she's kind of a geek.

Once again, the girls' table erupted in laughter. Lucas tried to catch Zoey's eyes, but she was far too engrossed in whatever they were talking about.

Lucas turned to the slop on his plate. *"Girl talk."* He didn't envy them for it. Whatever it was, he probably wouldn't want to hear it, anyway.

Two

Benjamin Passmore jerked awake in a cold sweat. His heart was hammering. Where was he? He gripped the sheets, struggling to orient himself. He'd just had a dream . . . he was a little boy, playing with Nina and Claire and Zoey, but for some reason, he couldn't see their faces. . . .

Suddenly he remembered where he was. He was at home in bed. It was Monday morning. Well, maybe not morning at this point. His alarm had gone off at the usual time, but he had quickly decided that he didn't have the energy or desire to go to school today. Thankfully, Zoey and his parents had offered no argument. They'd just left him alone.

He exhaled deeply. The intense and terrifying atmosphere of the dream had abruptly faded, leaving him once again in total darkness. *I should have savored that dream*, he said to himself in an empty, silent voice. *The only chance I ever get to see is when I'm asleep.*

With a violent motion, he threw the covers aside—then reached up and clumsily felt for the power button on his stereo. He needed to find out what time it was. He'd probably have to wait twenty minutes before somebody actually *said* the time. Until then, he'd just have to sit there.

". . . . WTOP news time, twelve-ten," a woman's crisp voice announced. "In national news, the president announced—"

Benjamin immediately flicked the stereo to the CD function. Today he'd been lucky. How long would he have had to wait if he had turned on the radio a second too late?

The mournful drum and piano opening to John Coltrane's *My Favorite Things* poured softly from the speakers. It was perfectly appropriate—dark and low and uncertain. He sat still for a while, losing himself in the sound. Unfortunately, the song soon shifted to a major key and the mood became bouncy and full of life. It was sickeningly upbeat, in fact. He didn't need to listen to that right now. On second thought, he didn't need to listen to anything. He fumbled once again for the button. With a click, the music fell silent.

"What to do, what to do," he said out loud. His stomach growled. *There* was something he could do. He could eat.

After putting on the new pair of Ray-Bans that Nina had bought him for his birthday, he pulled on his bathrobe and headed for the kitchen.

At least he still felt reasonably in control when he was in his own home. He hardly even needed to count his paces; the distances were so firmly ingrained. And when nobody else was around—asking him how he was *feeling*, if he *needed* anything—well, then, he didn't need to worry about accidentally bumping into anyone, either.

He turned left when he entered the kitchen and opened the refrigerator door. His hand curled around the handle of the orange juice pitcher. He lifted it, then frowned. For some reason, he had expected the pitcher to be heavier. He shook it once. It was empty.

All at once, rage engulfed him—instantaneously and uncontrollably.

"Dammit!" he shrieked out loud, hurling the pitcher to the floor. "Why didn't they make me any more orange juice? What am I supposed to do? How am I supposed to eat breakfast! I'm . . ." He tried to seek comfort in the sound of his own screaming voice, but it was useless. There was nothing he could do.

He forced himself to take a few quick breaths. He was trembling. Okay, so his parents or Zoey had forgotten to make more orange juice before they left. It wasn't a big deal. Rationally, he knew he shouldn't be angry. After all, they were only human. Unless, they had *purposely* not made him any juice, to teach him some sort of lesson. . . .

There was a loud pounding on the door.

Scowling, Benjamin walked into the hall. "Who is it?" he barked.

"Kate," a small voice replied. "Kate Levin." The voice sounded out of breath.

"What do you want, Kate?"

"I, uh, just wanted to see if everything was, uh—okay," she stammered uncomfortably.

Benjamin strode to the door and opened it. The cold early March air felt good. "Why wouldn't everything be okay?" he asked.

"Look, I know it's none of my business, but I was just out on the Cabrals' back porch—and I really know I shouldn't have been looking, but I could see into your kitchen." She spoke so fast that her rambling sentence sounded like one long jumbled word. "And then I saw you drop something and I heard you yelling and so I thought . . ." Her voice suddenly trailed off.

Benjamin chewed his lip. He could feel his face getting red—partly from shame and embarrassment, and

17

partly from anger. So the Cabrals' houseguest had witnessed his pathetic little fit. And naturally, since the poor, helpless blind boy was probably alone in the house, she had assumed the worst. He couldn't believe it. What was his life coming to?

"Are you all right?" she asked when he didn't say anything.

"Yeah, yeah, I'm fine," Benjamin said. "Uh . . . thanks for stopping by," he forced himself to add.

He didn't hear her move.

"Is that all?" he asked, a little more curtly.

"Look, Benjamin . . . I also wanted to thank you in person for what you all did for me on Friday night. You guys are so sweet. I mean it. You didn't have to ride to the hospital with me. It was totally unnecessary. And considering that it was your birthday and all . . . I just really, really wanted to let you know that it meant a lot to me."

Once again, Benjamin could feel his face getting hot. He'd been so completely self-absorbed that he'd forgotten all about Friday night. Well, he could at least console himself with one thing: he probably couldn't sink any lower in Kate's eyes than he just had.

"It was nothing," he finally managed. "I mean, it was the least we could do." He tried to smile. "How are you feeling?"

"I'm fine, I'm fine." She laughed. "It's actually been a great excuse for me to take the day off from school."

Benjamin nodded. *I know what you mean.* He sensed a slight, jerky movement. Then he realized what it was: she was shivering.

"Do you want to come in for a second?" he asked.

"Not if you're too busy or anything."

"No." He shook his head slowly. "I could, uh . . . use the company." *And I'd also like the chance to show*

18

you that in spite of everything you've seen, I'm really not a total jerk. He stood aside and closed the door behind her.

"Are you sure you're okay?" she asked as she followed him into the kitchen.

"Yeah," he said. "I just dropped the orange juice pitcher. I took it out of the fridge and I wasn't expecting it to be empty—so I, uh, yanked it a little too hard." He sat down at the table in the breakfast nook and grinned lamely. "Does that make any sense?"

"Sure," she replied. Her voice was relaxed—friendly and easygoing. He heard her reach down and scoop the pitcher off the floor. "Is there any more concentrate?" she asked. "I could make you some more."

"I . . . uh . . . don't know." The truth was that it hadn't even *occurred* to him to look for more concentrate. If it had, he could have made the juice himself. But his first and only reaction had been to throw a temper tantrum. It was ridiculous. "Here," he said, "let me get it." He stood up and took the pitcher from her, then opened the freezer door. Sure enough, his fingers brushed over several cans. "Have a seat."

"Thanks." She sighed. "So, look . . . I hope you were able to celebrate your birthday again this weekend. I mean, without all the . . ." She let the sentence hang.

"Violence?" he finished dryly for her.

She laughed. "Yeah."

"Kate, really—I'm just glad you're okay. To tell you the truth, I wasn't really in a party mood to begin with." He turned on the sink faucet and ran a can of concentrate under some hot water, then peeled back the seal. "You know, actually, in a weird way, it was kind of fun."

"Uh-oh. I hope that doesn't mean I'm going to have

to jump in front of somebody's fist at *all* of your parties."

"No, no. I'm sorry . . . that didn't come out right. I guess what I meant was that Chatham Island usually isn't so exciting." He dropped the concentrate into the pitcher, then filled it with water. "The most excitement we get around here is when Lucas's dad catches a halibut that weighs over eighty pounds."

"You don't find that exciting?" she asked sarcastically.

"Sure—*I* do," Benjamin said. "But I'm just a country bumpkin."

"Well, I want to be one, too." She sighed. "Seriously. You guys are so lucky to live here. I could easily see spending the rest of my life on Chatham Island."

Benjamin shrugged. He stirred the juice slowly, then turned to face her, pointing his Ray-Bans in her direction. He felt a sudden need to make "eye contact"—to prove to her, as he had proved to everyone in the past, that he was perfectly capable of handling himself like a sighted person. For the first time in a long, long while, he actually felt pretty good. With Kate, it was as if he were starting fresh, with a completely blank slate.

"I don't know," he said after a moment. "A city person like you might get a little stir crazy. This island is pretty small. Only three hundred people live here full-time."

"Yeah, but that's what's so cool. It's like a family. Everyone here is so *nice*. Nobody's afraid to look you in the eye or just wave and say hello, even if you're a total stranger. I mean, I'm used to keeping my head down and avoiding strangers at all costs. You always have to be suspicious in New York." She paused for a moment. "You never know if the person looking at you on the subway might suddenly leap out and stab you or something.''

Benjamin grinned. "Yeah, but *here* you have to worry about whether that person might suddenly leap out and punch you in the face.''

"You have a point there,'' she said. Benjamin could tell by the sound of her voice that she was smiling.

"Let me ask you something,'' he said. "Were you ever stabbed in New York?''

"Uh . . . I don't *think* I ever was.''

"But you've already been punched here.''

She laughed. "Your point being?''

"You see, we're *not* that different from city people. Everyone here has their seamy and violent underside, too. We just hide it under that small-town New England charm.''

"Jeez . . . what a cynic,'' she teased. "Look, Benjamin—you can try all you want to convince me that you Chatham Islanders are cruel and depraved, but I'm not buying any of it. Believe me, nobody in New York would have taken me to the hospital. I doubt if anyone would have seen me to the front door. They would have been like, 'Yo, later, babe. Try not to get blood on the floor on your way out.' ''

Benjamin started to laugh—but he stopped short. He felt a strange emptiness in the pit of his stomach. *Nina.* He almost said her name out loud. Everything about this conversation reminded him of the way he used to talk to Nina. That's because it felt so easy and familiar. But he hadn't had a conversation with Nina like this since the operation—because he'd driven her out of his life.

"Speaking of seeing me to the front door,'' Kate continued cautiously, "who was it that carried me out of your house that night?''

Benjamin shrugged, shaking any thoughts of Nina

21

aside. "Um . . . I'm not sure. It wasn't Lucas?"

"No," she answered distractedly. "Whoever it was stopped my bleeding with a piece of their shirt. You didn't happen to catch a glimpse—" She stopped in mid sentence.

All the short-lived happiness swiftly drained out of him, as if a plug had been released. "How would I have caught a glimpse?" he snapped.

"Benjamin, I am so sorry," she whispered shakily. "It's just that talking to you, I totally forgot . . . I wasn't thinking—I mean, the way you . . . it's just—"

"Yeah, well try not to *forget* in the future, all right?"

She didn't reply for a moment. "I'm so sorry," she finally repeated.

Benjamin ran a hand through his hair. He was trembling. Why was he even mad at her? Wasn't the fact that she'd forgotten he was blind a form of a compliment? Didn't he *want* everyone to think of him as Benjamin Passmore, the Blind Wonder Boy, the kid who can make you forget he can't see? Two months ago he probably would have *laughed*.

"Listen, I better go," she said. "I'll see you later, okay?"

He opened his mouth, but found he couldn't speak. He just couldn't apologize to her. *Nice going*, he said to himself. He listened to her footsteps, followed by the sound of the front door gently closing. *There's one more person you've managed to shut out of your life.*

He shook his head.

So much for showing Kate Levin he wasn't a jerk.

Three

"Hey, McRoyan!"

Jake was standing in front of his locker when he heard the gruff voice call his name from down the hall. He rolled his eyes. It was Coach McNair—the baseball coach. Coach McNair wasn't exactly Jake's favorite member of the Weymouth High faculty. He was a sadist when it came to coaching. He also had the added benefit of being an absolute moron.

"McRoyan—I've been lookin' all over for you," he said, pushing his way through the swarm of kids to where Jake was standing.

"What's up, Mr. McNair?" Jake asked. He brushed back his short, wiry brown hair and tried to appear as upbeat as possible. He even looked Coach McNair in the eye, which meant looking down at him. The guy was pretty short, not to mention strange looking. He was only about five foot five, with pale, freckled skin and flaming red hair.

"You get that permission slip signed yet?"

Jake's eyes narrowed. "What permission slip?"

"The one about baseball camp?"

"I . . . uh . . . don't know what you're talking about," Jake said confusedly. "I never got a permission slip."

Coach McNair frowned. "I gave everybody on the

23

team a permission slip. You must have lost it.''

Jake opened his mouth—but thought better of it. *No, I didn't lose it, you idiot; you forgot to give it to me.* Finally he took a deep breath. ''You're right. I must have lost it. What's the permission slip for?''

''The team's going to Florida for spring break. If you want to go, I'm gonna need that permission slip signed by your parents. By tomorrow morning at the latest. If I don't have it, you can kiss your starting position goodbye.''

You'd just love that, wouldn't you, Jake thought. ''Well, like I said, I don't have the slip,'' he said. ''Can I get one from you?''

Coach McNair shook his head disgustedly. ''You really don't have the slip?''

How many times do I have to say it? Jake shook his head.

''All right, McRoyan. Come with me. I'll give you one right now.'' He started down the hall.

The bell suddenly rang.

''Uh—my French class is about to start, Coach.''

Coach McNair whirled to face him. His eyes were blazing.

''You wanna go to Florida or not?'' he yelled.

Jake didn't answer. Maybe he *didn't* want to go to Florida. He could think of better ways of spending his spring break than hanging out with Coach McNair— like scrubbing toilets in the locker room, for instance.

''If you quit standing there and get your butt in gear, you'll get to class on time.''

Jake sighed, but he followed. He knew he couldn't afford to miss this trip. Of all the sports he played, he loved baseball the most. The guys on the baseball team were by far the coolest. Besides, this would be his last chance to play baseball at Weymouth High—ever.

Come to think of it, there was also another reason he needed to go on this trip. It would enable him to get far, far away from Lara McAvoy for a week. She *still* clung to the crazy hope there was something between them. He didn't know if everything was over completely, for good—but until she sobered up, he wanted nothing to do with her.

Coach McNair closed the door behind them when they reached his tiny office. After rummaging through his cluttered desk, he yanked out a sheet of yellow paper and jerked it in Jake's direction.

"Both your parents gotta sign this," he said. "Tonight. You understand, McRoyan?"

Jake took the paper and nodded.

"Don't lose it."

"I won't, Coach." Jake put his hand on the doorknob.

"Wait a sec, McRoyan."

Jake bit his lip. "I'm really kind of late, Coach."

"Class can wait. This is serious."

Jake bent his head. *Great. Just great. This is exactly what I need right now—some lame-brained pep talk about motivation while I'm missing a pop quiz.*

"Look at me," Coach McNair commanded.

Jake slowly turned to face him.

"I had an interesting little talk with your football coach this weekend. And guess what. Your name came up."

Jake felt the blood draining from his face. This was the same coach who had suspected Jake of using drugs. The coach who had let Jake off the hook this fall, even though he had played a game completely wired on cocaine.

"Any idea why your name came up, McRoyan?"

Jake shook his head.

Coach McNair put his hands on his desk and leaned forward. "I think you're lying," he hissed. "I think you know perfectly damn well why your name came up."

Jake swallowed, but he remained motionless.

"I'm just gonna say this to you once," Coach McNair whispered harshly. "I will not tolerate any druggies on my team. You got that? If I even *suspect* something, you're outta there. Do I make myself clear?"

Jake nodded.

"Well I'd like to believe you, McRoyan. I really would. But just to make sure, I'm asking everyone on the team to submit to a mandatory drug test at the end of the trip. That okay with you?"

"Yes, sir," Jake answered.

"I didn't hear you."

"Yes, sir!" Jake shouted. He realized he was clenching his fists so tightly that his fingernails were starting to dig into his palms.

"Good." Coach McNair slumped into his chair. "Now get going. You don't want to miss French."

As fast as he could, Jake turned and slammed the door behind him. He immediately bolted down the hall. His breath came in short gasps. He was sweating. Who the hell did Coach McNair think he was anyway? He had no right to talk to Jake like that. No right at all. . . .

His pace began to slow as he approached his classroom. The hall was empty now; the period had already started.

For some reason, a memory was flashing through Jake's mind—a very clear memory of *last* year's spring training, when the team had gone down to North Carolina. He and a few of the other guys had snuck away from the hotel on the last night and bought a couple of cases of beer. They had gotten totally plastered.

It had been a lot of fun. At least, what he had remembered of it.

Now he was having another memory—a memory of an AA meeting.

"Alcohol hardly ever shows up on a drug test. You have to be drunk while you're taking it." Some shaky, old lifelong alcoholic had said that. He had been describing how he used to sneak drinks at work.

No doubt some kids on the team would know this interesting little tidbit of information about drug testing as well.

Jake stopped walking altogether. He felt sick.

Drug test or no drug test, his teammates would be drinking down in Florida. It didn't even matter that he would be far from Lara. He would be tempted by alcohol. He knew it.

And the problem was that Jake would be all alone. He wouldn't have his parents, or his friends, or AA. And that meant he wouldn't have Louise Kronenberger.

Would he be able to say no if she wasn't around?

He could picture her face—her long blonde hair and seductive blue eyes. He had become used to seeing her every single day at those meetings. For a while, at the beginning, he had even thought he might have been interested in her. They had gone out on an awkward date. But they both realized that their relationship was far too fragile—and precious—to complicate it with any kind of romantic involvement. In a way, ever since he had joined AA, Louise Kronenberger had become his best friend. Now he wouldn't see her for an entire week.

"Come on, McRoyan, one beer ain't gonna kill you," his teammates would be saying. *"Just a little sip. What are you scared of?"* He could hear their voices as clearly as if they were right in front of him.

Suddenly he had an overwhelming desire to talk to Louise. As soon as possible.

Claire

Whenever I think of the word "friendship," I automatically think of Zoey. Nobody else I know is more worried about being a good friend than she is. Of course, she isn't as perfect as she would like to be. After all, she _did_ cheat on Lucas. But she tries. And I have to admit, as much as it gets on my nerves sometimes, and as much as I tease her about it, I really do value her friendship. In fact, I'd probably say that if I had to choose a "best friend," she'd be the one.

But I'm not really concerned with having a best friend. Anyway, I know that Zoey is a lot closer with my sister than she is with me. That's understandable. Nina's more needy than I am, and a lot more vulnerable. She's lucky to have a best friend like Zoey.

I guess I'm just not social in ways that most other girls my age are. I consider a lot of the activities that go along with "friendship" to be a waste of time—things like chatting incessantly on the phone or shopping for lingerie at the mall together. I'm sure it's fine for a lot of people. Just not for me.

So, how would I define friendship? That's a good question. I can certainly define what it <u>isn't</u>. It isn't cheating on you behind your back with some boarding school floozy who happens to be at a party.

What else?

It isn't making other people feel stupid. Nor is it lying, pretending to be something that you aren't, deliberately

hurting people, or ruining someone's
dreams.

So I guess I'd have to say that
friendship has nothing to do with Aaron
Mendel.

Four

As soon as Claire got home, she knocked on the door to her father's study. She didn't even bother taking off her knapsack. Now was as good a time as any to take care of getting permission to go to Miami—especially since Nina had decided to take a later ferry with Zoey. She didn't expect much resistance if she was in a one-on-one situation with her father. The simple fact was that Claire was a lot better at talking her father into certain things than Nina.

"Hi, Claire!" her father said. "Come on in, honey."

Claire opened the door. She silently groaned. No wonder her father sounded so chipper. He wasn't alone. Sarah Mendel—the happy-go-lucky midget—was with him.

"Hello, dear," Sarah chirped.

Claire plastered a smile on her lips. "Hi, Sarah," she said politely. In spite of the initial disappointment, Claire realized that Sarah's presence could possibly help her cause. She *did* have a frighteningly saccharine effect upon her father. He rarely said the word "no" when she was around.

It wasn't that Claire was particularly excited about spending a week with all the Island kids on some crowded beach in Florida. In fact, she would have much preferred staying at home the whole time and watching the weather patterns from her widow's walk. The problem was that Aaron was planning on spending *his* spring break in this house as well. And being with him in the same place at the same time, very simply, was intolerable.

"Dad, I have a question for you," she announced.

"What is it, Claire?"

"Zoey and Benjamin are planning a trip to Miami for spring break, and I was wondering if Nina and I could go along."

Her father peered quizzically at her over his reading glasses. Okay, so she had stretched the truth a little by saying that Benjamin had also been involved in the plan—but it wasn't an unreasonable thing to say. Mr. Geiger considered Benjamin Passmore to be the model of responsibility. And since Benjamin would end up going *anyway* . . . Claire figured it wouldn't hurt to throw in his name as well.

"A trip to Miami?" he asked. His tone was more somber than she had hoped for. "This is a little unexpected. Spring break starts Friday, doesn't it?"

"Yes, but—"

"How would you get there?"

"Well, Zoey's going to drive the Passmores' van. I was hoping you'd let us take our car as well."

A little half smile formed on Mr. Geiger's lips. "Oh you were, were you?"

"A trip to Miami!" Sarah suddenly exclaimed. "Oh—that sounds like fun!"

Claire suppressed a laugh. *Thank you, Sarah.* She did come in handy every now and then.

"Yes, I suppose it does," Mr. Geiger said thoughtfully. "Where would you stay? Have you thought about this at all?"

"Dad—we wouldn't even be leaving until Saturday. There's plenty of time to figure it all out. Listen, this trip would mean a lot to me. It *is* my senior year. This is probably the last time I'll get to do something like this with all my friends for a while. Maybe even forever."

Mr. Geiger chewed his lip thoughtfully. "Hmmm." He glanced at Sarah. "Well, considering you're going to be graduating this year . . ."

"Oh, Burke, let her go," Sarah said, putting her hand on his knee. "It sounds wonderful."

Claire couldn't help but smile.

"I guess you're right." Mr. Geiger cleared his throat. "It's too bad for Aaron, though. I know he was looking forward to seeing you."

I'll bet he was, she thought darkly. *He was probably looking forward to seeing Kate, too. At least she'll be around to entertain him.*

"I've got a great idea!" Mrs. Mendel cried all of a sudden. She turned to Claire. "Why don't you take Aaron along with you?" Claire nearly shrieked. It took every ounce of concentration to maintain an even facade. "Well, to tell you the truth, Mrs. Mendel," she said quickly, "we were kind of hoping this would be a chance for us Island kids to just get some quality time alone, you know. . . ."

Mrs. Mendel made a sad little face. Claire felt like punching it.

"But Aaron *is* an Island kid," Sarah protested.

"Really, Claire," Mr. Geiger said sharply. "What kind of answer is that? He's family."

Claire licked her lips. She had to think fast. "Well, you know, it's really not my decision to make. I don't know how Zoey and Benjamin would feel about it. . . ."

Mr. Geiger frowned. "Claire—"

"Oh, I don't want to cause any problems," Sarah interrupted. She shook her head and smiled. "I understand perfectly. I just know Aaron would have been happy to see you." She shrugged. "Who knows? Maybe he'll make some last-minute plans with some of *his* high school chums."

Chums? Claire cleared her throat. It was time to go in for the kill before her dad could argue any further. "Maybe he will. Look, thanks a lot, Dad. I really appreciate it. We're going to have a great time." She turned and made a hasty exit from the room.

"If you really expect to take my car, we have a lot of talking to do," he called after her.

"I know," she answered as she headed up the stairs. She allowed herself a little smirk. She would map out every single second of her vacation for her father if he wanted—just as long as she would be far, far away from Aaron Mendel.

"Hey, Benjamin—I'm home," Zoey called as cheerfully as possible when she walked in the front door. It was a little past seven o'clock. Zoey couldn't believe Benjamin had been here—*alone* in the house—all day long. It was too depressing to think about. She glanced at his door. It was closed, but she could hear soft jazz music coming from behind it.

She gave her standard knock: three short taps. "Can I come in?" she asked.

"Sure," came the dull reply.

Steeling her resolve to keep smiling no matter *what* Benjamin said or did, Zoey pushed the door open. She froze. Lara was sitting on the edge of Benjamin's bed. What was *she* doing here? Lara hadn't been in this house since their father had kicked her out, nearly two months ago. She was dressed in a tight little black T-shirt and jeans and her bleached blond hair had been cropped short. She was holding a paperback book—a translation of Jean-Paul Sartre's *No Exit*.

Benjamin was lying on the floor at Lara's feet. He was still in his bathrobe. His dark hair was a rumpled mess. He looked terrible.

"Uh—hi, Lara," Zoey finally managed.

Lara didn't even bother to look up from the book. "Hi, Zoey."

Benjamin tapped Lara's shin. "Go on."

"Okay . . . where were we?" she said absently.

"We were just at that line where Garcin says, 'Hell is other people.' " He laughed. "You know, I never realized what an astute observation that was—"

"I thought Nina read to you," Zoey blurted.

Benjamin propped himself up on his elbows, his expression sour. Lara kept her eyes fixed on the book.

"Not anymore," Benjamin stated. "Look Zoey—do you mind? I've got a lot of catching up to do."

"You'd probably do a better job catching up at school, don't you think?" she snapped. She couldn't help herself. *So much for the smiling*, she thought wretchedly.

"Listen," Lara said, snapping the book shut. "Maybe I better go. . . ."

"You don't have to go anywhere," Benjamin said. He kept his Ray-Bans aimed steadily at Zoey's face.

"No, really. I'm supposed to be at the restaurant soon anyway. Dad would be psyched if I was early." Lara quickly jumped off the bed and brushed past Zoey. "Bye, Benjamin," she called, grabbing her coat as she hurried out into the hall.

The front door slammed shut.

"Nice going, Zo," Benjamin said flatly. "How am I supposed to finish the play now?"

"I'll read the stupid play to you!" Zoey shouted. "Just stop acting like a baby!"

Benjamin's mouth opened slightly, but nothing came out. His lips quivered.

All at once the phone started ringing.

"Oh, jeez . . . ," Zoey mumbled. She stormed out of the room and into the kitchen, where she picked up the phone in the middle of the second ring. "Hello?"

"Guess what?" Nina's buoyant voice gushed. "Claire convinced my dad to let us take the car to Miami. The only thing is, he made us promise that we would stop halfway—"

"Nina, can I call you back?" Zoey interrupted.

"Uh, sure . . ." There was a pause. "What's wrong?"

"Take a guess."

"You told Benjamin about the trip?"

Zoey laughed shortly. "Not even. I barely said hello."

"What's going on?"

"To tell you the truth, I'm not sure. I'll call you back when I figure it out."

"Uh, okay," Nina replied. "Call me as soon as you can."

No sooner had Zoey placed the phone on the hook than it started ringing again.

"What the—" She furiously snatched the phone back up. *"What?"* she barked.

"Uh . . . Zo?" Lucas's voice asked hesitantly.

Zoey sighed. "Sorry," she muttered. "Hi."

"What's wrong?"

"Nothing. Just that Benjamin and I are in a fight, and the phone's been ringing off the hook—and the incredible thing is, I've only been home for about four seconds."

"Oh. Well, if it's any consolation, I think your voice is amazingly sexy when you're all riled up."

Zoey rolled her eyes—but she ended up smiling in spite of herself. Trust Lucas to come up with the lewd comment that would make her feel better. "Thank you," she finally said. "I *think.*"

"What's up with Benjamin?" he asked. "Can you talk about it?"

"Believe me, it's not worth getting into. I'm really glad you called, actually. I have something I want to ask you."

"Uh-oh. I don't like the sound of your voice."

"No, no. It's nothing bad." She tried to lighten her tone, but she ended up sounding completely phony. Oh, well. There was no use trying to sound enthusiastic when she was feeling exactly the opposite. "Lucas, do you want to go to Miami for spring break?"

The line was quiet.

"Lucas?"

"*That's* your question?"

"Yeah."

He started laughing.

Zoey frowned. "What?"

"Nothing, nothing. It's just that you sound so thrilled about it. Do you have to go to a funeral there or something?"

"I *am* thrilled about it," she said, ignoring his bad joke. "You just caught me at a lousy time."

"Oh." He took a deep breath. "Well, of course I want to go to Miami for spring break. There's only one problem. My dad."

Zoey held her breath. Lucas's dad was a "problem," all right. Until now, she hadn't even considered the possibility that Lucas wouldn't be able to come—but the thought of Mr. Cabral made that possibility seem more than likely. As far as Zoey could tell, his sole purpose in life was to make sure that Lucas remained perpetually miserable.

"You know what?" he said after a minute. "I bet if Kate came along with us, my dad would say yes."

"Kate?" Zoey swallowed. That wasn't exactly the solution she would have considered first. "But isn't she in college? Won't she have classes?"

"Her spring break is the same as ours."

"You really think she would want to come? I mean, she practically just got here. She hardly knows us. You think she would want to spend—"

"You don't want her to come," he stated, cutting her off.

Zoey fiddled with the phone cord. "I didn't say that."

"Zoey—I thought you said you didn't have a problem with Kate anymore."

"I *don't*," she mumbled unconvincingly.

"Good," Lucas said. "Because I want her to come. And I think she would be psyched. Besides, it would be a good way to make up for the fact that I punched her lights out."

Zoey laughed. "Yeah, I guess you're right about that. . . ."

"Cool. Then it's settled."

She raised her eyebrows. "Well, you do have to *ask* her, you know. And your dad."

"Yeah. I'll call you back as soon as I find out, okay?"

"Okay," Zoey murmured reluctantly.

"I love you."

Zoey smiled again, in spite of herself. "I love you, too."

"Talk to you later." The line clicked.

Zoey stared at the phone for a minute, then shook her head and hung up. It was amazing how three stupid little words could make you feel so wonderful—especially when the rest of your life seemed so lame.

All right, already. Let's wrap it up.

Jake fidgeted anxiously in the folding metal chair, listening to some guy named Victor drone on and on about how his wife had found his secret stash of vodka bottles in an army trunk. Normally, Jake would have listened carefully to every word. But tonight he had way too much on his mind.

He stole a furtive glance at Louise, sitting across the circle from him. She was staring intently at Victor. Jake still hadn't had a chance to talk to her all day. He hadn't seen her at school, and she had arrived late to the meeting.

". . . so that's when I finally gave up," Victor said. "I told her, 'Take these bottles and chuck 'em. I'm checking into rehab.' I've been sober ever since." He sunk back into his chair.

Everyone in the room applauded.

Finally, Jake thought, clapping along with the rest of them. He could tell from some of the pained expressions in the room that most of them were as bored as Jake was. He looked at the clock on the wall at the back of the room. It was already past eight o'clock. Not only was he bored—he was also starving half to death.

"Thank you, Victor," Dave, the group leader, said. "I know we ran a little late tonight, so I'll let you go. I'll see you all tomorrow."

Chairs scraped on the floor as people rose to leave.

"Louise," Jake called. He headed to intercept her at the door. "Wait up."

"Hey, Jake." She smiled, then looked at him more

39

closely. "What's up?" she asked in a hushed voice. "You look upset."

"I'm kinda freaked out right now, actually," he whispered. He took her arm and led her down the hall.

"It's not serious, is it?" she asked worriedly.

"I'm not sure." He waited until they had left the school building and were out in the chilly Weymouth night air before he continued. "I—uh—have to go away for a week."

She brushed her long blond hair out of her face and peered at him for a moment. "Jake, you haven't . . ." She didn't finish.

"Not yet." He glanced around, pausing until everyone who had been at the meeting was well out of earshot. "But I'm kind of worried. I have to go on this spring training trip with my baseball team to Florida. Last time I went, I got drunk. A lot of kids on the team drink."

She nodded gravely. "Can you stay in a separate place or something?"

He shook his head. "No way. The coach is already suspicious of me, and that would make him even *more* suspicious. We all have to stay in the same place."

"Why don't you talk to Dave about hooking up with an AA group while you're down there?" she suggested. "I'm sure he knows of one."

Jake thought for a moment. He could just see the scene unfolding: *"Hey, McRoyan, where the hell do you think you're going?"* Coach McNair would ask. And Jake would answer: *"Oh, nowhere, Coach. Just an AA meeting. Is it cool if I skip practice today?"*

"What are you thinking?" Louise asked.

Jake shook his head. "I don't think I would be able to get to a meeting even if I knew where one was," he said. "We're with the coach all day. The only time we're alone is late at night, in the hotel."

"And that's when the booze comes out," Louise said quietly.

Jake nodded.

For a moment, the two of them were silent. Jake shivered as the ocean wind blew across Portside. Even with Louise there beside him, he felt very cold and alone.

"I have an idea," she said. She turned her face into the wind and her long hair streamed behind. "Whenever you're by yourself at night, just head to the nearest phone and call me. We'll talk until you're ready to crash." She gave him a wry smile. "I'll bore you to sleep."

He laughed once. "Yeah. Sure."

"I'm serious, Jake."

He looked at her dubiously. "Louise, you want me to call you every single night?"

She shrugged. "Why not?"

"Well for one, the phone bills will be like—"

"Use One-Eight-Hundred-COLLECT," she interrupted. "I keep seeing those TV commercials and now I want to try it out. I guess television has that effect on me."

"You really want me to call you every single night," he repeated.

"Jake, we're not just talking about *you* here, you know. How do you think *I'm* gonna feel not having you around for an entire week?"

Jake just stood there, staring at her idiotically. He had no idea how to respond.

"So it's settled, all right?" She stuck out her hand. "Deal?"

He took her hand. He was already beginning to feel much, much better. "Deal."

"Good," she said matter-of-factly. "Now let's go get something to eat. I don't know about you, but I'm about to pass out."

41

Aisha

I think the most important part of friendship is acceptance. Everybody has faults, so you just have to accept people for who they are. If you respect someone, he or she will respect you back. There's a line in a Langston Hughes poem that sums up that philosophy perfectly. "My motto, as I live and learn: Dig, and be dug, in return." Needless to say, Langston Hughes was a lot more hip than I will ever be.

When I first arrived on Chatham Island, I worried a lot about being accepted. It wasn't easy being the "new girl in town." Everyone sort of gave me the cold shoulder at first. At the time, I wondered if it was because I was African American. As I soon learned though, race had absolutely nothing to do with it. It was just that they didn't consider me a full fledged "Island kid," because I didn't grow up here. In short, they were being snobs.

I guess my point is that even the

nicest, most considerate people have their hang-ups. Likewise, the most asinine people have some good qualities. Take David Barnes, for example. I mean, that guy has to be one huge, conceited pig if he thinks I actually enjoyed being kissed by him in front of everyone at the library. David Barnes is a dork. On the other hand, he is smart, and kind of funny. And slightly attractive, in a weird kind of way—although I would never tell him that.

The bottom line is that I can look past David's myriad problems in order to accept him as a friend. But that's it. He's nothing more. I mean, he doesn't even come close to being like Christopher, who's passionate, strong, witty, romantic, devastatingly handsome... about as close to perfect as a man can get. In fact, when it comes to Christopher, I can pretty much think of only one fault.

He joined the army.

Five

Aisha stared despondently at the tablecloth while her mother cleared the dishes and whistled happily to herself. For some reason, her mother actually *enjoyed* activities like cleaning dishes. She had this weird, compulsive need to always be doing some kind of chore. It was no surprise that the Bed & Breakfast was so scarily efficient.

"Dad, can I be excused?" Aisha's little brother asked. "I need to get started on my math homework." Kalif smiled at Aisha. "David's gonna be here soon," he said in an obnoxious, sing-song voice.

Aisha shot him a dirty look.

"Sure," Mr. Gray replied absently. He had already put on his glasses and was reading the paper.

Aisha still couldn't believe that David was actually Kalif's math tutor. It was a nightmare. Not only was David spending way too much time in this house, but Kalif had taken to telling him every little detail about Aisha's life. One of these days she was going to kill her little brother.

"What's wrong, dear?" Mr. Gray asked, glancing at her over the top of the paper. "You've hardly said a word all evening."

"I . . . uh . . . I guess I'm just kind of nervous about

winning that prize," she lied. "I find out the results of the test on Thursday." She *was* nervous about the prize, but that wasn't why she was feeling so gloomy. When she had gotten home, her mom had told her that Christopher had tried calling her. Unfortunately, there was no way she could call him back. The base wouldn't allow incoming calls for people in basic training.

"I'm sure you did fine," her father comforted. "Besides—it's not like you have anything to lose. Try not to think about it." He chuckled. "After all, spring break is right around the corner."

Spring break. Aisha immediately perked up. She'd been so depressed over missing Christopher's call that she had forgotten to ask her parents about the trip. "Speaking of spring break, I had something I wanted to ask you."

"What's that?"

She took a deep breath. "Well, Zoey and Claire and Nina are planning this trip to Miami Beach, and I was wondering if I could go along."

Mr. Gray folded the paper and put it down, wrinkling his brow. "A trip to Miami Beach?"

Aisha nodded, smiling.

"Does this mean I would have to buy you a plane ticket?" he asked soberly.

"No, no. They're going to drive. They're taking two cars."

"Two cars? For four girls? Two cars seems a little excessive."

Aisha blinked. Sometimes she just didn't get how her father's mind worked. Why would he get hung up over the number of cars they were taking?

"Well, there would be more than four of us going," she said. "I mean, Benjamin and Lucas and Jake would probably come, too."

"Boys?" Mr. Gray's expression grew even more serious. "I better get your mother. Carol," he called loudly.

"What is it?" she answered from the kitchen.

"Come here for a minute, please. Aisha has an interesting proposition."

Aisha swallowed. *An interesting proposition?* It wasn't as if she was asking if they thought she should sleep with Robert Redford in exchange for a million dollars.

Mrs. Gray appeared in the doorway. "Yes?"

"Aisha wants to drive to Miami Beach with some boys," he said.

"Dad!" Aisha yelled. "That's not what I said at all, Mom. Zoey and Nina and Claire are driving to Miami Beach for spring break. Jake and Lucas and Benjamin— whom you know very well—are going with them. I'd like to go, too."

Mrs. Gray looked concerned. "Would all of you be staying in the same hotel?"

"Of course we would!" Aisha cried. "Jeez, Mom— you let Christopher stay in the B&B for a while. I mean, he and I were practically roommates."

"That was different," Mrs. Gray replied. "He was injured, and he had nowhere else to go. Besides, your father and I were here, too."

Aisha let her hands flop down on the table. "Fine. I'll stay in a convent. How's that?"

Her father laughed. "Not such a bad idea."

She shook her head. "I can't *believe* how ridiculous you guys are. Those boys are my *friends*. You *can* have friends who are members of the opposite sex, you know."

"We're not saying you can't, dear," her mother said. "But I think your father and I would like to know more

46

of the details. We'd probably like to discuss it with the Geigers and the Passmores as well.''

"Fine. Can I just get a tentative yes or no first?"

Her parents exchanged a long glance. Finally her father said, ''Well, if it's all right with the other parents—''

"Thank you." Aisha stood up from the table, exasperated. ''Now if you'll excuse me, I also have some homework I need to do."

Before her parents could say another word, she marched through the foyer and into her room. She shook her head with a snort. Her mother and father were absurd. They acted as if they lived in Victorian England or something. Why couldn't she have *cool* parents, like the Passmores? The Passmores probably spent their evening telling Zoey and Benjamin about all the crazy things they did on *their* road trips.

She collapsed onto her bed. There was no point obsessing about it. She had gotten permission—well, *almost*—and that was the important thing. She picked up the phone next to her bed and punched in Zoey's number.

After two rings, there was a click. "Hello?" Zoey answered. She sounded half asleep.

"Hey, it's me."

"Oh. Hey, Eesh," she said tonelessly.

"Gee, Zo, it's nice to hear your voice, too."

"Sorry," Zoey grumbled. ''It's been sort of a long day."

"What's up?"

"Benjamin and I aren't speaking. What's up with you?"

"Whoops." Aisha cringed. "I'm sorry—"

"Don't worry about it, Eesh." There was a warning

note in her voice. Aisha got the subtext. *"Don't pursue that line of conversation, Eesh."*

"Well, I've got some good news," Aisha said, with as much cheer as she could muster. "I think I'm going to be able to go on the trip. My parents want to talk to your parents about it first, though."

Zoey laughed dismally. "Yeah, well this trip is shaping up to be a little less than what I originally expected."

"Uh . . . what do you mean?"

"I'll tell you what I mean. Here's the final lineup: you, me, Nina, Claire, Lucas, and Kate."

"Benjamin isn't going?"

"Barring a minor miracle—such as him regaining his vision in the next four days—I'd have to say no," Zoey said.

Aisha paused for a second. That was an unusually harsh thing to say—particularly for Zoey. Things must have *really* been bad over there. She sounded as if she'd given up on him completely. "Well, uh, what about Jake?" Aisha asked.

"I just got off the phone with Mr. McRoyan. Jake has to go to baseball camp."

"Whew." Aisha shook her head. "So *Kate* is going?"

"Yup. Lucas didn't waste a second inviting her along."

"Hmmm. Well . . . that's cool, I guess."

"It is?"

"Yeah. You don't think so?"

"No . . . I guess you're right," Zoey said dubiously.

"Come on, having Kate along won't be so bad. She seems really nice, actually. I mean—especially the way she handled getting punched in the face. I don't think I would have been as polite about it."

"Yeah. I'm just a little worried about how Claire is going to react."

"Uh-oh." Aisha twirled the phone cord around her fingers. "I didn't even think about that."

"Neither did I, at first. But somehow I've got a feeling that *I'm* going to be the one who breaks the news to her." Zoey sighed. "Look, I can't really talk right now. I haven't even started my homework yet. I'll see you tomorrow, okay?"

"Okay. Bye." Aisha placed the phone back on the hook.

She rubbed her eyes for a moment, then sat up straight. Poor Zoey. That girl had become a serious magnet for bad luck recently. And the sad thing was, bad things only seemed to happen to her when she was trying to help other people out.

But Aisha wasn't exactly free of bad luck herself. She glanced at the phone again. She couldn't believe she had missed Christopher's call. She'd give anything just to hear his voice. . . .

The doorbell suddenly rang.

Aisha's heart bounced in her chest. David was here. And she did not need to hear *his* voice right now. Without hesitating, she leapt up, turned off all the lights in her room, and locked her door.

"Hi, David," she heard her mother say. "Kalif's up in his room."

"Thanks, Mrs. Gray."

Aisha held her breath as his footsteps slowed in front of her door—then continued on up the stairs.

She let out a sigh of relief.

Wait a second, she said to herself angrily. *What am I doing? Why am I hiding in the dark from some loser who I don't even like? What am I afraid of?*

But even as she asked herself these questions, she

knew very well what she was afraid of. She was afraid that David Barnes might try to talk to her, to smile at her—maybe even try to kiss her again.

And she was even more afraid that she might try to kiss him back.

When Claire was certain everyone else in the house had gone to sleep, she bundled herself up in a sweater, scarf, and hat, and headed up the tiny ladder to her widow's walk.

The air was crisp and quite cold—but it was invigorating. It would help her think. And she had a great deal of thinking to do.

For a moment she stood still and gazed out at the ocean. The moon was almost full. It was pretty amazing how bright the light was, actually. She would easily be able to see well enough to write in her journal.

After rubbing her hands together, she leaned around the chimney and pulled away the loose brick that concealed her diary. She began writing immediately.

Temperature: 38 degrees. Winds 7-to-10 mph. A cloudless sky. The forecast looks good for the next few days. Daytime temperatures may even reach 50.

Well, well. It's been an interesting few days.

Ever since I found out that Aaron is really a two-timing sleazebag, I've been racking my brains to come up with a plan that will split our parents apart. I can't bear having him be a part of my life. That goes for the midget, too, for that matter. She's starting to seriously drive me up the wall.

Today, thanks to Zoey's brilliant idea of going on a group vacation, I came up with a plan. I just needed that little push in the right direction. If all goes well, my dad will be asking Sarah to move out by the time I get back from a week of sun and fun in Miami.

And why?

Because he's going to get a very suggestive little letter.

Sarah loves collecting the mail every day. I have no idea why. Maybe it makes her feel as if she's making herself useful around the house. She always sorts through the letters and opens them for my father. Personally, I think it's interfering, but my dad seems to like it.

So on our journey south, when we need to stop at a gas station in say, Maryland or North Carolina, I'm going to drop a little note in the mailbox.

It will probably go something like this:

Dear Burke,

I've been thinking about you so much. Ever since you stopped in (place name here), I haven't been able to get you out of my mind. I know you're involved with another woman, but we have a love that will not die. That brief night of passion we had in (place recent date here) will be forever etched upon my mind.

*Please don't hate me for writing you,
Burke. Just know that I love you, and that
I cannot forget you.
Love,
(Place sexy name here)*

Claire put the pen down and rubbed her hands together again. Her wrist ached from writing so fast. But she felt good. She knew she would have to put a lot more time and energy into the letter than she had tonight. But in the next week, she would craft a masterpiece. Burke Geiger would receive the love letter of his life. The postmark from some exotic Southern locale would prove its authenticity.

And Sarah Mendel would read it first.

Claire rubbed the sides of her arms vigorously, then shoved the diary back in its hiding place. She needed to get to sleep. Tomorrow was going to be the first of a series of busy, busy days before she left.

Six

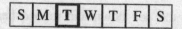

On *Tuesday* Jake dropped off the signed permission slip in Coach McNair's office, first thing in the morning. On the way out he happened to bump into his good buddy Tad Crowley, notorious party animal and starting second baseman on the baseball team. Tad told him in hushed, secretive tones not to sweat the drug test. There would be plenty of fun in Miami. He was going to make sure of it.

Benjamin finally decided to go to school. Most of the Island kids avoided him. After each class, he met with his teachers and promised them he would make up his missed assignments by the end of the semester. On the ferry home that afternoon, Zoey worked up the courage to ask him if he wanted to go to Miami for spring break. He refused, saying he had too much work.

On *Wednesday*, Mr. Gray called the Passmores to talk about "the logistics of the trip." Mr. Passmore assured Mr. Gray that Zoey had already found a place to stay—the Park Central—and that the boys would be sleeping in separate rooms. He added that from what Zoey had told him, it looked as if only one boy would be going, anyway.

When Mr. and Mrs. Passmore came home from the restaurant that night, they both gently urged Benjamin to join the rest of the kids on the trip. He told them he would think about it, but he had a lot of work to make up. Before he went to bed, he called Kate and apologized for snapping at her. She told him she had already forgotten about it, then asked if he was coming on the trip.

S	M	T	W	**T**	F	S

On *Thursday*, Aisha found out the test results: she and David received the exact same score. Westinghouse needed some time to make the decision on what to do with the prize money. David seemed very pleased. He said that "great minds really do think alike." Aisha spent the rest of the day avoiding him.

That night, Benjamin finally agreed to go on the trip—provided that Lara could go, too. Zoey tried to argue. Benjamin said it was too late; he had already asked Lara to come along. Too fed up to put up a fight, Zoey said that Lara was welcome to come, provided that they ride in separate cars.

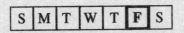

S	M	T	W	T	**F**	S

On *Friday* Zoey broke the news to Claire, Aisha, and Nina that Lara would be joining them, too. She still hadn't told Claire that Kate was coming, of course. She would tell her this afternoon, when they all went to do some last-minute shopping at the mall. Or maybe she would call her that night. Either way, she would make sure to tell her.

Benjamin took the ferry home from school with Lucas and Jake. They talked about Miami. Jake said that the baseball team was staying at some hotel called the Park Central in South Beach. Lucas said he was pretty sure that *they* were staying at a place called the Park Central, too. Jake smiled tepidly. What a coincidence. Benjamin asked Jake if he knew that Lara was coming. Jake didn't. He begged them not to tell her that he was staying in the same hotel.

Late that night, Claire finished the final draft of the phony love letter on her computer. She printed it out, then carefully wrote in the signature that she had practiced on a separate sheet of paper. She was very pleased with herself. In a few short paragraphs, she had embodied the perfect mix of subtle suggestiveness and pining lust. If meteorology didn't pan out, Claire figured she might have a future writing romance novels.

Last-Minute Purchases

Claire

1) One box of pink Cartier stationery and envelopes
2) One black Donna Karan bikini
3) One bottle of Coppertone sun block, level eight

Nina

1) One carton of Lucky Strikes
2) Two tapes: *The Miseducation of Lauryn Hill* and the Foo Fighters' *The Color & The Shape.*
3) Two pairs of four-dollar sunglasses
4) A baseball hat with the logo: *I'm not a tourist, I live here!*
5) A "family pack" of Twinkies

Zoey

1) One bottle of Coppertone sun block, level four
2) The latest issue of *Seventeen*, with the feature story: "Sex: It's Worth Waiting For"
3) A pair of shorts for Lucas

Aisha

1) A deliberately unrevealing one-piece green bathing suit
2) The latest issue of *Mademoiselle*, with the feature story: "Long-Distance Relationships: Making Them Work"

Nina

How would I define friendship? Easy. Friendship is telling somebody who just tipped the scales at four hundred that she looks exactly like Kate Moss. That's all there is to it, really.

You see, friendship has this problem: it's always doomed to fail. I know that sounds a little pessimistic, but I can't help it. I'm speaking from personal experience. Other people seem to have better luck, though. Take my sister, Claire, for instance. She's been buddies with Lucifer for her entire life, and their bond just seems to grow stronger every day.

So why am I so down on

friendship? Well, to begin with, my two closest friends, Zoey and Aisha, are graduating in about three months. That means that they will soon go to college, where they will meet new and exciting and sophisticated people . . . and after about two weeks they'll both be like, "Nina _who?_"

That leaves my other best friend. Make that _former_ best friend. Yes, Benjamin—who may or may not be graduating this spring as well—has dumped me. Plain and simple. He just dropped me like a bad habit. Left me out with yesterday's trash. And so on. (Sorry, I'm too depressed to complete the rule of comic tautology right now.)

The thing that hurts most about my break-up with Benjamin is that I just never imagined not being friends with him. I mean, I was always worried that he might meet somebody more beautiful, more intelligent, and more glamorous than me. But I never considered the possibility that we wouldn't be friends. No matter what happened, I always thought there would be some kind of rapport between us.

But, hey—enough of my yacking. All this talk is making me want to hurl. I guess I have a lot to learn about friendship. The problem is, they make it look so easy on "Friends."

Seven

"Nina—get up," Claire was muttering. "Come on, move it."

Nina groaned and rolled over, pulling the pillow over her head. She felt as if there were lead weights attached to her eyelids. It couldn't be time to get up yet. Hadn't she only just gone to sleep?

"Come on!" Claire whispered fiercely. "It's six forty-five already. They'll be here any minute."

"Five more minutes," Nina croaked. "Five more . . ."

Before she knew what was happening, Claire had yanked the pillow off her head and was smacking her face with it. Nina snapped awake.

"All right!" she yelled crossly. "I'm up! Leave me alone!"

"Ssssh," Claire hissed, knitting her eyebrows. "Don't wake up Dad and Sarah." She tossed the pillow onto the foot of the bed and left the room.

Nina shook her head. Good old Claire. Her older sister was a delightful breath of fresh air first thing in the morning. She glanced out the window at the lighthouse, perched on a rocky shoal a little ways from the island. The sky behind it was a deep, deep blue, tinted with a faint hint of pink. The sun had barely risen. It was *way* too early to be getting out of bed on a Saturday morning.

After yawning for about ten seconds straight, Nina finally forced herself to move. She almost tripped over her suitcase as she stumbled for the bathroom. Luckily, she'd been smart enough to pack the night before. Knowing how scattered her thoughts were in the morning, she probably would have ended up packing her ski boots and an overcoat.

"Hurry up," Claire huffed. She shambled past Nina in the hall, struggling with a tote bag, a knapsack, and two suitcases. "The ferry leaves in less than fifteen minutes."

"I *know*," Nina mumbled. Her voice was still hoarse. She watched as Claire hurried down the stairs. Why did Claire always bring so much *stuff*? She looked as if she had packed for a month—not a week.

Nina shook her head. Hopefully the rest of them weren't as cranky as she was. This was going to be a *long* drive. She headed for the bathroom and fumbled for the light switch.

"Ugh," she said out loud.

The face that stared back at her from the mirror certainly didn't do a whole lot to lift her mood. Dark circles ringed her eyes. Did she look that bloated and pasty *all* the time? Her matted brown hair was sticking out in uneven clumps. She grimaced. It wouldn't do any good to worry about it. Besides, who did she have to impress, anyway? It wasn't as if she had a boyfriend or anything.

A week in Florida will do wonders for me, she consoled herself as she squeezed some toothpaste on her toothbrush. *I'm going to swim four miles every single day, eat nothing but fresh fruit, and*—

The faint sound of a car horn honking made her jump.

Uh-oh. Nina immediately spit out her toothpaste and

dashed back into her room, wrestling herself into the first pair of black jeans she spotted on the floor. She would just wear the T-shirt she had worn to bed. As fast as she could, she laced up a pair of high tops and pulled on her leather jacket.

Claire's footsteps thundered up the stairs. A second later, her annoyed face appeared in Nina's doorway. "Nina—"

"I know, I know." Nina scooped her suitcase on the floor and hurried from the room.

The two of them nearly slammed into her father and Sarah in the hall. So much for not waking them up. Nina suddenly realized that they were wearing *matching* pajamas. She forced herself to smile.

"Have fun, you two," Mrs. Mendel said, grinning broadly.

"We will," Nina replied as she followed Claire down the stairs. "Thanks. Bye."

"And call as soon as you get to the hotel," Mr. Geiger called after them. "I want to know that you made it there in one piece—"

"Bye!" Nina closed the door behind her.

For some reason, Claire wasn't moving. She was standing in front of the house with her arms folded across her chest, staring blankly at the Passmores' van. Maybe she was looking at Lucas's surfboard, strapped precariously to the roof. From the way it was hanging there, Nina could easily picture it flying off on the highway and slamming into some car—namely her father's Mercedes. Oh, well. There was no point worrying about it before they got on the road.

"Come on," Nina urged. She yanked open the door of the Mercedes and threw her bag into the backseat. She still couldn't believe that Claire had convinced their father to let them use his car. Maybe Claire really *did* have evil powers.

"What the hell is *she* doing here?" Claire suddenly barked.

Nina turned to see Claire thrusting a shaky finger at one of the van windows.

"Oh, no," Nina breathed.

Kate Levin was behind the window, looking horrified. Zoey must have conveniently forgotten to tell Claire that Kate would be joining them.

Zoey rolled down the driver's side window. Her lips were pressed into a tight line.

"She's coming with us," she said simply, glaring at Claire. "Now let's go."

Claire wouldn't budge. "Not with me, she's not."

"Fine," Zoey snapped. "But our van is too crowded. You have to take Lara."

"I'm going to ride with Lara, too," Benjamin piped up from the backseat.

Claire shook her head. "You really screwed up this time, Zoey," she said disgustedly. "You really did."

Nina rubbed her face with her hands. This couldn't be happening right now. "Look, Claire," she said, grabbing her bag out of the car. "Benjamin and Lara can ride with you, and I'll ride with Zoey, all right? We have about three minutes to make the ferry."

Without another word, Claire stormed over to the Mercedes and shut herself with a loud *thwack* into the driver's seat.

Nina opened her mouth, but she realized there was nothing more to say. They had to get moving. She watched numbly as Lara leapt out of the back of the van and helped Benjamin maneuver over to the Geigers' car.

Part of her was hoping that Benjamin would suddenly

change his mind—that he would suddenly stop and say, "Hey, wait a second. I don't want to ride with my deranged half sister after all. I think I'll ride in the van, with Nina." But she knew that was about as likely as Claire saying that she had changed her mind about Kate.

Well, she'd been right about one thing.

This was going to be a long drive.

Eight

That morning . . .

Benjamin wasn't a huge fan of silence. But he'd been sitting in Claire's car now for what seemed like an eternity, and neither Claire nor Lara had uttered so much as a peep. Not that he liked mindless chatter, necessarily, but he liked *some* conversation—especially if there wasn't any music. The only sound was the steady purring of the *Island Whisper's* motor as it carried them slowly to Weymouth.

Finally he cleared his throat.

"You know, I haven't been on the *Titanic* in almost three years," he said.

"The *what*?" Lara asked.

"It's a nickname for the car ferry. You know, like the way we call the regular ferry the *Minnow*?"

Lara responded with a grunt.

Benjamin slouched back in his seat. So much for mindless chatter. This was going to be miserable.

"I can't believe Zoey," Claire murmured. Benjamin could tell she was talking to herself more than to anyone else. "What was she thinking?"

"What's the deal between you and that girl, any-

67

way?'' Lara asked. ''Did she fool around with your boyfriend or something?''

Oh, no. Benjamin wished he could just melt into the upholstery. At least he was sitting alone in the backseat. He was beginning to think that maybe it would be a good idea if he just hopped out of the car in Weymouth and came right back to Chatham Island.

''It's none of your damn business, Lara,'' Claire said icily. ''So don't ask.''

''Ooh,'' Lara replied in a spiteful, mocking voice. ''Tough girl. Hey, look, can we put some tunes on or something? I'm getting bored.''

''Benjamin?'' Claire asked.

He swallowed. ''Yeah?''

''Would you like to hear some *tunes*?''

''Why not?'' He was pretty sure he would hate whatever Lara wanted to put on—but that was okay. At this point, anything was preferable to talking.

''Kate, I am so sorry about what happened back there,'' Zoey suddenly announced. She looked in the rearview mirror. Kate was squashed in the backseat between Nina and Aisha. They had been sitting wordlessly in the bowels of the *Titanic* ever since they had gotten on board. ''It's totally my fault. I should have told Claire—''

''Don't worry about it, Zoey,'' Kate gently interrupted. She flashed her a conciliatory smile. ''Besides, you're wrong. It wasn't *totally* your fault. None of this would have happened if I hadn't hooked up with Aaron.''

Zoey nodded. Kate had a point. Whenever anyone hooked up with Aaron, it quickly ended up in catastrophe. She cast a quick glance at Lucas in the seat beside her. He was staring out the window at nothing, his face grimly set. Even hearing Aaron's name seemed to infuriate him. Of course, that was perfectly understandable.

"Uh, Zo?" Nina asked hesitantly. "Mind if I ask you a question?"

Zoey met Nina's gaze in the mirror. "Why didn't I tell Claire that Kate was coming?"

"How'd you guess?"

Zoey pursed her lips. "Would *you* want to tell Claire that Kate was coming?"

Nina sighed. "You've got a point there."

"I really don't want Claire to hate me," Kate said quietly. "I feel so bad. . . ."

"Don't worry about Claire," Lucas said. "She'll get over it. She always does."

"That's right," Nina said dryly. "By the time we get to Florida, Claire will be back to her normal bubbly self."

That afternoon . . .

As soon as the tape was over, Claire breathed an exaggerated sigh of relief. The music sounded like somebody being tortured with a bunch of jackhammers. She immediately pushed the eject button.

"Hey!" Lara protested. "That was only side one."

"Tell me you're not serious," Claire groaned.

Lara shook her head. "Man, I can't believe you guys. You don't like *Back in Black*? It's a classic."

"A classic," Claire repeated. She had been gripping the steering wheel so tightly that her fingers were starting to ache. She glanced at the gas meter. The tank was almost empty. They would have to pull over pretty soon. Maybe then they could ditch Lara. Or at least trade her for somebody halfway normal from the other car. Even Kate might be preferable at this point.

"Hey, do you mind if we listen to something a little more mellow for a while?" Benjamin asked from the backseat.

Claire smiled. "I thought you'd never ask."

"You should've told me you didn't like it," Lara grumbled.

"We were being polite," Claire replied. "You should try it sometime, Lara. It actually feels pretty good."

"Come on, Claire," Benjamin said tiredly. "Can we just try to have a friendly, normal conversation?"

Claire glanced in the rearview mirror. Benjamin was looking extremely unhappy. For a moment, she almost felt bad. "Fine by me," she said, softening her tone. "Let's have a friendly, normal conversation."

"About *what*?" Lara muttered.

"How about what we're going to do down in Florida?" he suggested.

Lara snickered. "I bet that's what they're talking about in the other car. Zoey's probably planning out a whole schedule for us. She's always gotta be the mother hen."

"Well, what are *you* going to do, Lara?" Claire demanded. "Just take it whichever way the wind blows?"

"Something like that," she said. She chuckled to herself. "I think I am gonna try to watch a couple of baseball games, though."

Claire frowned. What was *that* supposed to mean? There was just no understanding the girl. She was a total lunatic.

"My butt's asleep," Nina said for what seemed like the hundredth time. "I've got fanny fatigue."

"We *know*, Nina," Aisha said, squirming in her seat. For the past two hours, she'd been carrying on a silent

70

battle with Kate over seat territory, and now she was starting to lose. Her entire body was mashed up against the side of the door.

"Can we please talk about something besides our butts?" Zoey asked. "This is getting ridiculous."

"Maybe we should talk about when we're going to pull over next," Aisha said. She was beginning to feel a little light-headed. The only food she'd had so far all day was a jumbo coffee and one of Nina's Twinkies. She had tried to read *Mademoiselle*, but it had made her too dizzy.

"I think we should talk about who's gonna ride shotgun next," Nina said, pulling a Lucky Strike out of her T-shirt pocket and shoving it in her mouth. "I vote for me."

Lucas laughed shortly. "Too bad your vote doesn't count. Kate, what do *you* want to talk about?"

Kate lifted her shoulders slightly. "Um, actually, talking about who gets to ride shotgun sounds like a good idea to me. . . ."

"Don't worry," Zoey said. "I'll pull over for gas soon. Then you guys can fight it out."

Nina leaned across Kate and snatched the *Mademoiselle* out of Aisha's lap. "Well, until then, I think I can find something that will entertain us." She grinned as she flipped through the magazine, letting the unlit cigarette dangle from her lips. "They've always got some kind of interesting quiz in here. . . ." She turned the pages more slowly, then stopped. "Ah, yes. Here we are. Perfect. The title of this quiz is 'Are you a good girlfriend?' "

"Nina?" Lucas said. "I'll tell you what. I'll let you ride shotgun if you agree to put that magazine away—"

"No, no. It's important for you to hear this, Lucas. I

think this will reveal a lot about your relationship with Zoey. Here's a good one. 'When your mother criticizes your boyfriend at the dinner table, you A, agree with her and tell him to shape up; B, stare at your plate and pretend not to notice; C, stick up for him, but only after your mother has left the room; or D . . .' "

The more Nina read, the more depressed Aisha became. As stupid as the quiz was, she couldn't help being reminded of Christopher. Why would a question like that remind her of him? First of all, her mother had never criticized Christopher at the dinner table. In fact, she hardly ever criticized him at all. Of course, there wasn't anything to complain about. There wasn't anyone more gracious. . . .

" . . . Eesh?" Nina was asking.

"Huh?"

"A, B, C, or D?"

Aisha made a face. "None of the above."

That evening . . .

Lara was beginning to feel antsy. They were somewhere in Delaware now, and the ride had gone on long enough. She needed some relief.

"Hey, Claire?" she asked. "Uh . . . can we pull over? I really need to go to the bathroom."

Claire hesitated. "Yeah. We need to get more gas, anyway." She rolled down the window and waved at the Passmores' van behind them, signaling that they were going to make a stop.

Lara smiled as appreciatively as she could manage. The exit was just ahead. Now all she needed to do was figure out how she could bring her bag with her to the bathroom without arousing suspicion. She anxiously drummed her fingers on her knees. *I could say I wanted to brush my teeth*, she thought. That actually wasn't so far from the truth. She'd been eating junk food all day and she hadn't brushed her teeth once. It would feel good to clean out her mouth. *After* she'd had a little drink.

Claire slowed the car and pulled into the gas station just off the exit. "Hurry up," she mumbled, once they jerked to a stop.

"I will," Lara said quickly. "Uh—can you pop the trunk? I just want to get my toothbrush. My mouth feels kind of gross right now."

Claire gave her a strange look, but she obliged.

"Thanks." As quickly as she could, Lara leapt out of the car, grabbed her duffel bag, and followed the signs to the rest rooms in back of the gas station. Her face wrinkled when she pushed the door of the women's room open. The place stank. Oh, well. She'd gotten drunk in worse places.

Closing the door of the stall behind her, she tore into her bag and dug through her clothes. Her fingers touched the glass. *There you are.*

An unopened fifth of vodka. Sweet salvation. She yanked the bottle out and unscrewed the cap.

"Cheers," she whispered.

The liquor seared her throat as it went down ... followed by a terrific, nauseating jolt as it hit her stomach ... and then she smiled. Yes, that was good. She loved that initial *boom* more than anything—that burning fire that started way deep inside and spread out through her body, filling it with a delicious warmth. The trip wouldn't be so bad after this. In fact, she might even start to have *fun* for a change.

After a few more long slugs, she screwed the cap back on and shoved the bottle back into her bag.

Oh, yeah. She almost forgot. She still had to brush her teeth.

Lucas was very glad that Claire had decided to stop. He needed some fresh air. Being cooped in a van with four girls was beginning to wear on him. Now he knew what "girl talk" really was—nonstop gibberish. When they got back on the road, he was going to take the wheel and insist upon absolute silence.

As he headed around the back of the gas station, he saw Lara was coming out of the women's room. Her head was down.

"Hi," Lucas said.

She didn't seem to hear him. In fact, she seemed to be talking to herself. She kept walking and bumped right into him.

"Whoa!" she exclaimed. She staggered a little bit, giggling. "Watch it there, buddy."

"Sorry." It was *her* fault, but he really didn't care. He kept walking—then stopped. Something about the way she looked made him pause. Her face looked flushed, and her eyes were vaguely unsteady. "Are you feeling all right?" he asked.

"I'm feeling great! I'm psyched to hit the road."

Lucas nodded slowly. Psyched to hit the road? They'd been on the road for almost twelve hours already.

"So what's it like in your car?" she asked, breathing toothpaste into his face. "Our car's kinda boring."

Lucas shook his head. So *that's* why she was feeling great. She was drunk. "Yeah, well, I guess our car is kinda boring, too," he said quietly.

"Hey, what's the matter?" she asked. "You look bummed."

He laughed. "Do I? I guess I'm probably a little more

bummed than *you* are right now." He started walking again.

Suddenly Lara grabbed his wrist. "What's that supposed to mean?" she demanded.

He wrenched himself free with a violent twist. "What do you think it means?" he spat. "You're wasted."

"Ssssh!" she whispered. She looked nervously over her shoulder. "Shut up."

"Lara, if you're worried somebody's gonna find out that you've been drinking, why the hell did you get drunk in the first place?"

"For your information, I'm *not* drunk. But if your little Miss Perfect girlfriend finds out I had a cocktail, she might cause problems. Get my drift?"

Lucas just stared at her, his jaw tightly clenched. He'd never had any desire to punch a girl before. Of course, he was the only guy he knew who ever *had* punched a girl, but that was a little different. Then again, knocking out Kate had set a precedent, right?

"So I had a drink, Lucas," Lara muttered, brushing past him. "Big deal. It's nothing to get worked up about."

"Nothing to get worked up about?" he cried. "Man, you make me *sick!*"

She paused for a second, then whipped around to face him. "Chill out, all right? Just *chill out*. It's not like I'm hurting anyone."

"Yeah, that's a real easy excuse, Lara. Is that what you were thinking when you puked all over Jake's bathroom? That you weren't *hurting* anyone?"

She sneered. "Jake didn't care about that."

Lucas couldn't believe what he was hearing. Is that what she truly thought? "You're right, Lara," he said caustically. "You're absolutely right. In fact, Jake probably wants you to find him at the Park Central and puke all over his bathroom there, too.''

A sly smile slowly formed on her lips.

"What?" he demanded.

"I didn't know Jake was staying at our hotel," she said.

Lucas opened his mouth, but he suddenly felt queasy. "I . . . I . . ." he spluttered.

She winked at him. "Thanks for the info, sweetie." Before he could say anything else, she disappeared around the corner.

Lucas hung his head. Perfect. Why couldn't he learn to keep his mouth shut? How many stupid mistakes would it take?

A thought occurred to him then—one that made him feel even worse.

Jake is going to kill me.

Day Two

7:45 AM After spending the night in a Motel 6 outside of Richmond, Virginia, Zoey tries to wake everyone up. For some reason, Lara has a harder time getting up than everyone else.

8:03 AM Nina wants a chance to drive her father's Mercedes. Aisha, Lucas, and Kate decide they want to ride in the Mercedes as well. Zoey reluctantly agrees to let Benjamin, Claire—and Lara—ride with her.

10:26 AM Lara asks Zoey if they can pull over so she can go to the bathroom. She seems to be in a much better mood when she comes back.

11:14 AM Kate continues the *Mademoiselle* quiz where Nina left off yesterday. After much pressure, Lucas agrees to assume the role of the "girlfriend" for purposes of answering the questions. He scores a thirty-five out of a possible one hundred, placing him in the category of "Lost Cause—Should think about becoming a nun."

11:53 AM As soon as Lara starts snoring, Benjamin announces that he can smell alcohol on her breath. Zoey tells him that if he doesn't like Lara's drinking, he shouldn't have invited her along.

1:40 PM Aisha tries to write a letter to Christopher in the backseat of the car, but the bumps on the highway keep causing her pen to slip. She goes through seven pieces of Claire's brand-new stationery before she finally gives up.

2:27 PM Lara wakes up, groggy and irritable. She immediately asks Zoey if they can pull over again. Zoey tells her she's going to have to wait.

5:02 PM Both vehicles cross the Florida State Line.

5:04 PM Lucas's surfboard flies off the roof of the Passmores' van. Luckily, the highway is deserted. It takes twenty minutes to back up and strap it on again.

6:16 PM Aisha agrees to take the quiz. She scores a forty.

6:38 PM Claire suddenly realizes that she has forgotten to put the love letter in the mail. In a panic, she asks Zoey if they can pull over. They are just outside of a town called Vernon, population six hundred.

6:40 PM Upon further reflection, Claire decides that Vernon is probably not the most likely place for her dad to have an affair. She decides to mail the letter from Miami.

8:05 PM A fight breaks out at a roadside McDonald's over who is going to share rooms at the Park Central. Nina wants to be with Eesh and Zoey. Claire refuses to be with Kate. Kate says she doesn't care *where* she sleeps, as long as she has a bed—and offers to share a room with Eesh and Nina. Zoey refuses to be with Lara. Lucas quietly suggests that he and Zoey share a room, but is quickly shouted down. Finally, Nina agrees to room with Lara and Claire—leaving Zoey, Eesh, and Kate to share a room.

11:41 PM The Passmores' van and the Geigers' Mercedes pull into the Park Central Hotel. The hotel is right on Ocean Drive, across the street from South Beach. The weather is beautiful—breezy and in the mid-seventies. Nobody notices.

12:03 AM After Lara and Nina are asleep, Claire goes to the lobby to call her father. Yes, they made it in one piece. Before heading back up to the room, she drops the letter in the hotel mailbox.

The Letter

Dear Burke,

Forgive me for writing to you. I figured a letter would be better than a phone call. I had to do something, because I've been going crazy for the past six weeks. And the more I go over that night in my mind, the more I realize that we have to talk. Soon.

That morning when you left me, you told me that you probably would never be able to see me again—at least not in the same way. You were engaged. You had two daughters. You told me that in spite of what happened between us, you were still in love with her. You told me that it was a mistake, that it never should have happened, and that it would never happen again.

But it did happen, Burke. And I know that no matter how much you pretend, you can't deny it or wipe it from your memory.

I have no regrets. It was one of the most wonderful nights of my life.

Please write me back. I'm not expecting
any sort of decision, or any promises. I just
want to know that you still think of me.
Even better, call. I just want to hear your
voice.

Love,

Madeline

Nine

Zoey was the first to wake up. A few narrow shafts of brilliant sunlight were streaming through the heavy curtains of the hotel room. She glanced at the digital clock on the night table beside her. It was already almost ten o'clock.

She propped herself up in bed. This room was a huge improvement over the rooms in the Motel 6. It was about four times the size. Each of the massive double beds could probably sleep three people comfortably. As it was, she and Aisha had decided to share a bed, leaving Kate with one to herself.

The little bit of sunlight behind the curtains was so bright that she had to squint. Moving slowly and carefully so as not to wake Aisha up, she got out of bed and tiptoed over to the window.

The moment she pushed the curtain aside, she could barely keep her eyes open. In front of the hotel, just across the street, not fifty yards away, was South Beach. Zoey pressed her face against the glass and looked to the right and left. The sand stretched in either direction as far as she could see. Her jaw dropped slightly. She couldn't believe the color of the ocean. It was so *blue*—nothing at all like the dull green-gray waters that surrounded Chatham Island.

A burst of euphoria rushed through her. They were really in Miami. Already, the drive down was beginning to seem blurry and unreal. It was time to put the past two days behind them. It was time to get on with having some fun.

"Zoey?" Aisha's hoarse voice asked.

Zoey turned around and grinned. "You gotta check this out, Eesh. It's unbelievable. We are so psyched."

Aisha tossed the covers aside and staggered over to the curtains. "Man, oh, man," she breathed, squinting beside Zoey. "I never thought we'd make it."

There was a soft knock on their door.

Zoey glanced at Kate's bed. She was still dead to the world. Nothing was visible but her mop of long red hair. After the second knock, however, she began to stir.

"Coming," Zoey hissed. She walked delicately across the room and opened the door. Nina was standing there in a pair of cut-off fatigues, high-tops, and a T-shirt imprinted with the word "Anarchy." She was holding a hotel towel. She had probably forgotten to pack her own. Zoey smirked. Even if Nina spent the rest of her life in Miami, she would never become a "beach" person.

"What's up?" Nina asked loudly. "Have you checked out—"

Zoey immediately put her finger over her lips. "Kate," she mouthed.

"Oops," Nina whispered. "Sorry. I just wanted to know if you guys had checked out the view yet."

"Pretty sweet, huh? You ready to hit the beach?"

"Miami, here I come," Nina said dully.

"Where's Claire?"

"She and Lara are still asleep."

"That's cool. Let me just put on my bathing suit. It'll take two seconds."

Nina nodded. "I'll go see if Benjamin and Lucas are up."

Zoey hurried back into the room. Aisha's face was still pressed against the window. "You want to go to the beach?" she asked in a hushed voice.

"Nah. I thought I'd just sit in this hotel room all day and watch TV."

There was a rustling movement in Kate's bed. Kate stretched her arms over her head and yawned loudly. "You guys are going to the beach?" she asked groggily.

"Yup." Zoey reached into her bag and grabbed her bikini, a pair of shorts, and a shirt, then headed for the bathroom. "You want to come?"

"Hmmm." Kate licked her lips. "I think I'm gonna sleep for a little while longer. . . ."

"We'll be right out front," Zoey said, closing the door behind her. She glanced into the mirror as she got dressed. *Yuck.* Her skin was the same drab color as the bathroom tile. Maybe she would skip putting on the sun block today.

Benjamin heard the knocking on the door, but he decided to ignore it. If Lucas wanted to answer, that was fine. But he was just going to pretend he was asleep. He could tell from the sound of the knock exactly who it was. Nina.

After one more knock, her footsteps quietly faded away. Good. He was *not* going to spend his entire vacation hanging out with her. There was no law saying that *all* the Island kids had to hang out together *all* the time. Miami was a big city. And he fully intended to take advantage of it. He would go check out some Latin jazz, hear the Miami Symphony, try out some Cuban food. If the rest of them wanted to hang out on the beach and do nothing all day, then so be it. *He* wasn't here to get a tan.

There was only one problem.

Miami *was* a big city—and one with which he was totally unfamiliar.

It suddenly occurred to him that since he had gone blind, he had rarely ever left the confines of Chatham Island, except to go to school. Or to go on stupid little trips, like that time they had all gone skiing in Vermont. But on those occasions, he had willingly let other people take care of him. Back then he'd been the "Great Blind Wonder." Every once in a while people could take care of him, because the rest of the time he was so totally self-sufficient.

Of course, he didn't really qualify as "The Great Blind Wonder" anymore. Now he was more like "The Great Blind Loser."

I should have picked up one of those guidebooks in Braille, he said to himself. Since he hadn't, he would have to be dependent on someone while he was here. In fact, he would need someone just to tell him where he could eat or go to the bathroom. There was really nothing he could do by himself. Nothing at all.

He rolled over in bed. Hunger was picking at his stomach. If he could *see*, he could just get up and walk to the hotel restaurant. But that wasn't an option, was it?

"Lucas?" he asked tentatively.

There was no response.

He cleared his throat. "Lucas?" he repeated, this time with a little more force.

Still nothing.

"*Lucas!*" he shouted.

"Whassa?" Lucas gasped. "Wha . . . ?"

He took a deep breath. "Are you awake?" he asked quietly.

By the time Claire had managed to force herself out of bed and get dressed, it was already almost eleven o'clock. Nina was gone. Lara, of course, was still passed out. Not only that, but she was wearing the most absurd pair of polka-dot pajamas that Claire had ever seen. She must have gotten up in the middle of the night and changed into them. For all Claire knew, she had also gotten up in the middle of the night to do a couple of shots from whatever bottle was stashed in her bag.

Claire tossed a towel and suntan lotion into her tote bag and headed out into the hall. She had to admit it: Zoey had picked a winner. The hotel was a lot nicer than she'd expected. And in spite of the spring break crowd, Zoey had even managed to book three rooms next to each other—314, 316, and 318. All of them faced the beach.

Claire paused in front of 316, Lucas and Benjamin's room, then decided against knocking. Benjamin was probably in no mood for early morning chitchat. It would be better to check on the girls first.

There was a note on the door.

To Benjamin, Lucas, Claire, and Lara (and anyone else who happens to walk by):
We're at the beach right in front of the hotel. Come and join us ASAP!
Kate

Claire peered at the note closely.

A very strange, unsettling feeling swept over her as she looked at it—almost a sort of déjà vu. For some reason, she was certain she'd seen that handwriting before. Fairly recently, too. But where? Kate was staying at the Cabrals', and Claire hadn't been *there* in ages.

Aaron.

Of course. *That's* where she'd seen Kate's handwriting—in Aaron's room at Gray House, when he had stayed there over Christmas break. In one of her weaker moments, Claire had decided to do a little . . . *exploring.* Specifically, she had poked around his room while he wasn't around. And she had discovered a shoebox full of letters. One of the letters had been from a girl named Kate. *This* Kate.

Claire shook her head. She remembered the letter very clearly now, almost word for word. "*I know we were only together that one night and we were both pretty trashed, but it was nice. I don't know if you know this, but it was my first time.*" The rest of the letter wasn't so flattering. "*Don't worry. I mean, it was great, but it wasn't* that *great. No offense.*"

A quiet laugh escaped Claire's lips.

It was so strange. At the time, Claire had thought a lot about "Kate." In fact, she had pictured her looking like Nina. There was something irreverent and self-deprecating in the tone that had reminded Claire of her younger sister. The letter was pretty remarkable, actually, considering that Kate had lost her virginity to Aaron. Claire had left Gray House that day having a lot of respect for that girl—whoever she was. She never thought in a million years that she'd *meet* her—much less spend spring break with her.

Clichés always prove true, she thought. *It's a small, small world.*

Maybe she'd been a little harsh on Kate. There was really no reason *not* to respect her. It hadn't been Kate's fault that she thought Aaron was available. Aaron had done nothing to indicate otherwise.

Still, it was a little disconcerting that Kate had gone ahead and hooked up with him anyway. After all, Aaron wasn't supposed to be "that great," right? Claire wrinkled her nose. *She* had gone to that lame boarding school party fully intending to lose her virginity to him as well. Seeing this note, however, reminded her of exactly what she had missed.

Not much.

LUCAS

I'm the wrong person to ask about friendship. I don't have a lot of friends. But I'm not complaining. The fewer friends I have, the less likely I am to get into trouble.

Friends have always caused me problems. The most obvious example, of course, is Claire. There was something more than friendship between us, I guess— but whatever it was, it landed me in Youth Authority for two years and nearly got me disowned.

No . . . on second thought, I'd have to say that friendship had nothing to do with Claire and me. I'm not sure what that relationship was. I suppose it was blind loyalty and infatuation on my part. I still have no idea what it was on hers.

I think a big part of friendship is sharing something with someone else. Like advice, for example. I

mean, I always considered
Christopher to be a friend,
because we always ended up
telling each other about all
the miserable things that our
girlfriends did to us. I kind of
miss that, actually.

Okay, "miserable" is an
exaggeration. Even with the
problems and the arguments and
everything else, I'm still
completely in love with Zoey.
The good things about her far
outweigh the bad. We give each
other a lot and get a lot in
return. We have a true
friendship. Of course, I can think
of one thing we haven't given each
other yet, but that's another
story altogether.

The truth is, I'm perfectly
happy having Zoey as my only friend.
We understand each other. She
can tell what's on my mind
without having to ask me. That's
really important, I think.

So maybe I can answer the
question. Friendship, as far as

I'm concerned, is the
relationship I have with Zoey.
   I guess that means it would
really, really suck if we broke
up.

Ten

Lucas was bored. Well, a little more than bored. *Irritated*. There was only so much he could take of having to lie around the beach and listen to five girls jabber about all the amazing-looking guys in Miami. Especially if one of the girls happened to be his girlfriend.

"Hey, Lucas?" Nina suddenly asked. It was the first time anyone had bothered to acknowledge his existence in the last fifteen minutes. "Did Benjamin say when he'd be back?"

"No, he didn't," Lucas grumbled. "I told you, he didn't say anything."

"Oh, yeah. I guess you told me that."

Lucas kicked at the sand. This morning wasn't turning out quite the way he'd envisioned it. First off, Benjamin had woken him up and immediately demanded breakfast. Then he needed help putting his clothes away. Then he wanted to be dropped off at Lara's room. It wasn't that Lucas minded helping the guy out; he knew Benjamin was going through a tough time. He just didn't appreciate being treated like a personal manservant, without so much as a "please" or "thank you." It was particularly annoying given that everybody else was sitting in the sun and gawking at every single male who happened to walk by.

"Hey, Zoey?" Aisha said worriedly. "Maybe you should put some sun block on. I think you're getting burned."

Lucas glanced over at Zoey. She was lying facedown on a towel, sandwiched between Claire and Nina. Aisha was right. Zoey's normally pale back was starting to turn pink.

"Just five more minutes," Zoey mumbled. "I really want to get some color."

Lucas shook his head. Why was it that girls were so obsessed with how they *looked* all the time? He couldn't care less if Zoey had a tan. Who was she trying to impress—herself?

Finally he stood up and brushed himself off. "I think I'm gonna go try to find someplace where I can surf," he said.

Zoey looked up at him, shielding her eyes from the sun with her hand. "You can't surf around here?"

Lucas laughed. "Not unless I want to kill somebody. It's way too crowded. Anyway, the waves here are totally lame."

"Oh." There was something in Zoey's voice that silently added, *"Well, excuse me for asking."*

"You know, I've always wanted to try surfing," Kate mused, staring out at the ocean.

Lucas shrugged. "Why don't you come with me? I could teach you."

Kate laughed. "That's nice of you to offer—but you obviously have no idea what you'd be getting yourself into. I'm *really* uncoordinated. I won the award for 'Biggest Klutz' at my high school. They actually gave me a trophy. I'm serious."

"Come on—you can't be *that* bad." He beckoned to her. "Really. It'll be fun."

She raised her eyebrows. "You won't make fun of me?"

"Of course I'll make fun of you. That's the whole point."

"You make it sound so tempting," she said dryly.

"Come on, Kate," he urged.

"Well, humiliation *is* my favorite past-time . . . Okay. Why not. You got yourself a student. Let me just run up and grab my camera, all right?" She pushed herself to her feet and started trudging through the sand toward the hotel. "I want to get some action photos of the surf stud."

Zoey lifted her head. She opened her mouth as if she were about to say something—then closed it and put her head back on the towel.

"What?" Lucas asked.

"I wasn't going to say anything," Zoey replied innocently. "*Surf stud.*"

Lucas rolled his eyes. If Zoey was in one of those petty moods where she had to make a big deal about every stupid, meaningless little comment, he would be better off leaving her alone. "Uh, can I get the keys to the van, Zo?"

"Why do you need the keys?" she asked.

"Well . . . it's kind of hard to drive the van without the keys, don't you think?"

She glared at him. "I don't understand why you need to take the van."

"I just said—there's no place to surf around here."

"Yeah, but, I don't know if you should really be driving . . ."

"Zoey, give me a break!" he cried. "I drove practically all day on Saturday."

"Yeah, but that was different. I was in the car. Plus, it was on the highway."

"Look—why don't you just go with him?" Claire said flatly. "You'll get a tan no matter where you are."

Zoey rolled over on her back and squinted up at the sky. "Well . . . what if it clouds up while we're driving around looking for the best place to surf?"

"Not likely," Claire muttered. "There isn't a cloud in the sky. Besides, at this time of year, it never gets cloudy until the late afternoon. The rainy season—"

"Okay, Claire, that's fine," Nina interrupted. "We get the picture. We don't need a weather report from Chatham Island's leading meteorologist."

Lucas shifted on his feet impatiently. This whole situation was beginning to drive him crazy. "Zoey, are you going to come or not?" he demanded.

Zoey sighed. "Sure. I'd love to watch Kate learn how to surf."

"Hey, nobody's forcing you." He was about to add, *"Feel free to stay here and guy watch"*—but he thought better of it. Now was not the time to get into a full-fledged fight with Zoey. Especially since all her friends were beginning to exchange uncomfortable glances.

"I want to come," she said. She slowly got to her feet and stretched. Suddenly she winced. "Ow."

Lucas frowned. "What's the matter?"

"Nothing. My back just feels a little hot. . . . So, does anyone else want to come with us?"

Uh-oh. Lucas cast a quick glance at the rest of them. There was cranky Nina, with her ridiculous black T-shirt and face sopping with suntan oil; sour Claire (although she admittedly looked extremely sexy in her black bikini); and mopey Aisha, wearing some ludicrous green bathing suit that looked as if it went out of style in the fifties. *The fun bunch*, he thought miserably. *Please say no, please say no. . . .*

95

"I'll come," Aisha finally said.

"Anybody else?" Zoey prodded.

"Nah." Nina shook her head. "I think I'm gonna stick around here and get in some quality bonding time with dear old sis."

Claire didn't say anything.

"Sounds good," Lucas said quickly. "See ya." He turned and began marching through the hot sand for the hotel. Two out of three wasn't bad. It could have been worse.

"Hang ten, dude!" Nina shouted after him. "Ride the big blue tube! Surf or die!"

Lucas squeezed his eyes shut. No—it could have been *a lot* worse.

"I really, really hope you were joking," Claire said, once Aisha, Zoey, and Lucas were gone.

"Joking!" Nina exclaimed. "Come on. I want this vacation to be a special time for us, Claire." She sniffed and rubbed her eyes, pretending to weep. "I know they only say this in beer commercials—but I *love* you, man."

Claire's expression was stony. "Please go away, Nina." She glanced up at the sun, then repositioned herself so that she was facing the road instead of the ocean.

"But I'm having so much fun," Nina mumbled. She turned back toward the water. She wasn't exactly thrilled about having to hang out on the beach with Claire—but the alternative would have been watching Lucas and Zoey fight, or listening to Aisha lament over Christopher. Maybe she could just wander the streets aimlessly until she happened to run into Benjamin and Lara. Miami wasn't all *that* big, right?

A drop of sweat fell from her nose onto the sand.

"It's so *hot* down here," she said.

"Mmm," Claire growled.

For some reason, nobody else on the beach seemed to be sweating. Then again, nobody else looked like actual human beings. They all looked as if they had been churned out at some Ken and Barbie factory. Even if she had plastic surgery, breast implants, a liposuction, and four personal trainers, she would never look like these people. The best she could do was try to stave off skin cancer. She reached into Claire's tote bag and grabbed the suntan lotion. The bottle made a disgusting squirting noise as she squeezed it into her hand.

"Don't use that all up," Claire warned.

"I won't," Nina said. She slathered the white goo generously over her face, then squeezed out another glob. "Man—this stuff is gross."

"So don't use it."

"I have to use something."

"Why don't you just go inside? Then you won't have to use anything."

"But then I wouldn't be able to sit here and torment *you*, Claire. I have to get some sort of pleasure out of this vacation." Nina tossed the lotion into the bag and leaned back on her elbows. "If Benjamin were around, I could torment *him*, but—"

"Here he comes now," Claire said.

"Funny."

"I'm serious."

"You're going to have to do better than that."

"Take a look for yourself."

Nina turned around. Her heart lurched. Sure enough, the tall familiar figure in sunglasses and black pants was walking across the road, tapping a long, thin white cane in front of him. Lara was at his side, her arm intertwined with his.

"Over here," Claire called, waving.

Lara waved back.

"Oh, jeez," Nina breathed.

"I thought you *wanted* to see Benjamin," Claire said quietly. "You haven't stopped talking about him all day."

Nina kept her eyes pinned to the pair as they slowly made their way through the crowd. "Yeah, but, saying you want to see someone and actually wanting to see them are two totally separate things."

"Well, if you can, try not to act like a five-year-old," Claire whispered.

Lara and Benjamin stopped a few feet in front of them.

"What's up, guys?" Nina asked.

Benjamin twisted his lips. "Who's there?"

"Uh . . . just me and Claire," Nina said.

"Where's everyone else?"

"They all went to watch Lucas teach Kate how to surf," Nina said. She laughed nervously.

Benjamin nodded. His expression remained blank.

"Have a seat," Claire said.

"Uh, no thanks." Benjamin shook his head. "I'm too hot. I think I'm just gonna go inside for a while. I just wanted to hear the ocean."

Nina jumped up. "I'm hot, too. I'll go with you."

Benjamin's jaw twitched, but he said nothing.

"Well, *I'm* gonna hang here," Lara said. She let Benjamin's arm go and plopped down into the sand beside Claire. Almost immediately, she began pulling off her tight T-shirt and tiny little cut-off shorts, revealing an even skimpier bikini than what Claire had on. "I need to catch some rays."

Nina gently took Benjamin's arm. "You want to—" She broke off when she felt him stiffen.

"You really don't have to come with me, Nina," he said. "I can make it back to the hotel myself."

"So can I," she said. "That makes two of us."

"What I'm saying is—"

"Benjamin, don't flatter yourself. I'm not going back to the hotel because of *you*. We happen to get free HBO here, and *Porky's II* starts in five minutes. You *know* how much I love that movie."

For a fleeting instant, Benjamin's face showed the faintest beginnings of a smile—but then it hardened again. Nina sighed. At least his arm was starting to relax. She gripped it a little more firmly. "Now should we go?"

"Sure." He sighed. "I don't want you to miss the beginning."

"Is *Porky's II* really on right now?" Lara asked.

Nina blinked.

"Of course it is," Claire said, meeting Nina's bewildered gaze. "You think Nina would make something like that up?"

Nina shook her head, then quickly steered Benjamin back in the direction of the hotel. Lara McAvoy needed some serious help. Maybe all the booze had rotted her brain. Nina almost felt bad about leaving Claire alone with her. *Almost.* "Bye, you guys," she called.

"Have fun," Claire called back.

We'll try, Nina thought. She and Benjamin began walking in silence. After a few more seconds, his arm finally relaxed entirely. It wasn't much of a sign, but it was something.

For a moment, she could almost pretend that things were back to normal—that they were just taking a stroll, arm in arm, as they had so many times in the past. She wondered if he felt the same way. It felt so good to be next to him, touching him. . . .

"You know, you don't have to be so mean to Lara," Benjamin suddenly hissed.

She frowned. "How was I being mean to Lara?"

"You and Claire were making fun of her."

"*Claire* was making fun of her. Besides, I can't help it if Lara is an idiot."

"Dammit, Nina, she's *not* an idiot!" Benjamin whispered furiously. "It's just that nobody ever gives her a chance."

Nina took a deep breath. She was *not* going to get into an argument. "Fine. You're right. I was unfair. I won't make up stories about any of the *Porky's* movies ever again in her presence."

"Nina—"

"Look, forget about it, all right, Benjamin?" She paused when they reached the road, struggling very hard to remain calm. "Let's change the subject."

"Fine."

"Good. Let's talk about something pleasant. What did you guys do this morning?"

"We went for rice and beans at this Cuban restaurant Lara knows about." His tone was colorless. "*Carlita's.* It was really good."

"How did Lara know about it?" Nina asked. She looked both ways and started across the street.

"A friend of hers grew up in Miami."

"Excellent. Now, see—isn't this enjoyable? Having a normal, friendly conversation?"

Benjamin snorted.

"What?"

"Nothing. It's just that I said the exact same thing to Lara and Claire on the drive on the way down: 'Let's have a normal, friendly conversation.' Whenever you say something like that, you know that the conversation is going to stink."

100

Nina let his arm go. She didn't need to be subjected to his foul mood any longer. If he wanted to be left alone, that was fine with her. She had brought him across the street. The Park Central was right in front of them, its huge glass doors not twenty feet away. He could go the rest of the way himself. "Well, so much for small talk," she said. "Here we are."

He nodded, looking vaguely apprehensive. His cane bounced feebly on the sidewalk ahead of him. "I . . . uh, don't know where 'here' is."

A painful lump suddenly formed in Nina's throat.

Don't cry, she ordered herself, squeezing her fists into tight little balls. *Don't make a fool of yourself.*

"Nina?"

She drew in a deep, quivering breath. "You're right in front of the hotel," she managed in a strained voice. "The door's about twenty feet away. Dead ahead."

Once again, his face became an impassive mask. "Thanks. Look, I'm kind of tired, all right? If anyone asks, I'm just taking a little nap. I'll see you later."

She just nodded, not trusting herself to speak. Benjamin shuffled along slowly, tapping the cane in quick, rhythmic arcs on the paved walk in front of him. It seemed to take an eternity for him to reach the doors. When he was halfway there, a woman walked out of the lobby—then noticed him and stopped. She held the door ajar, patiently waiting for him to make it inside.

That should be me, Nina thought.

A tear fell from her cheek.

One of these days, Benjamin was going to realize what he was missing. He couldn't go on acting like this forever. He'd come back to her sooner or later—maybe not on this trip, but he definitely would. She was sure of it.

Wasn't she?

JAKE

How would I define friendship? I'm not really sure how to answer that question. I don't think friendship can be pinned down in any way. But I do think it starts with honesty. If someone is honest with you, then you can usually work through whatever problems might come up. At least, I hope so.

I guess honesty is so important to me because I've been lied to so much. My dad lied to me about his affairs. Wade lied to me about drinking. Claire lied to me about Wade. So did Lucas, for that matter. In a way, Lucas's lie was just as bad as Claire's. A lie that serves some sort of purpose, no matter how well-intentioned, is still a lie.

I should know. Alcoholics are good liars. I lied to everyone I knew, including myself. But you know what? It's amazing how good honesty can feel when you've lied for so long.

Maybe that's why I can relate to Louise so well. She and I are coming from pretty much the same place. We've got nothing to hide from each other. No secrets. That's why things are so easy between us.

I feel like that with Zoey, too. I know that she'll always be honest with me. She'll always look out for me. I can count on her. That's not to say we haven't been through our share of lies in the past. I mean, I'll never forget how I felt when she started falling for Lucas. But we worked through it. And I have to admit, as difficult as it is sometimes, that Zoey and I make better friends than we do a couple.

It's funny. Now that I think about it, I guess most of my friends—my real friends—are girls.

Of course, I can think of one girl who isn't. I'm not saying that Lara and I will never be friends—maybe we will someday. Just not now.

Unfortunately, she seems to have a tough time getting the picture.

Eleven

Jake had chosen a seat at the front of the bus, even though it meant sitting right across from Coach McNair. His head was starting to ache. Everybody seemed to be shouting at the top of their lungs. The plane had been bad enough, with people screaming and throwing napkins back and forth across the aisle. The situation had gotten so out of control that the stewardess had been forced to make an announcement. But in spite of all that—and in spite of Coach McNair's warnings that they could very easily just turn around and go back, "in the blink of an eye"—the team hadn't settled down.

"Hey, McRoyan!" Tad Crowley yelled from the back of the bus. "Your momma's so ugly, I hear she—"

"Crowley!" Coach McNair barked. He stood up and faced the rear. "One more peep outta you and we're turning this bus around. Do I make myself clear?"

Jake felt his ears get hot. He hated having Coach McNair stick up for him. But he just couldn't bring himself to say anything. In years past, he would have stood up and hurled an insult right back at Tad Crowley. Of course, in years past, he probably would have been sitting with him in the back of the bus.

I'm going to have to explain why I'm acting so weird, he thought dejectedly. *There's no way around it. I'm going to have to tell Tad and the rest of them that I've sobered up. The old Jake McRoyan is dead and gone.*

"What's the matter, McRoyan?" Coach McNair asked, sitting back down. "You feeling all right?"

"Fine," Jake muttered. "Just a little tired."

"Well, that's all right. We'll be at the hotel soon. After a good night's sleep, you'll be ready to go. We got a lot of work to do tomorrow."

Jake leaned against the window and stared out at the Miami skyline as they sped down the highway. The sun was already pretty low in the sky. Coach McNair was right. He just needed to get a good night's sleep.

Hopefully he wouldn't have any distractions.

It was bad enough that all the Island kids were staying at the same hotel—but far worse was that Lara would be there with them. He couldn't believe that they had actually *invited* her to go. Couldn't they see her for what she was? She didn't need a vacation; she needed help. He had given up thinking that a good person lurked somewhere inside her, just beneath the surface. She was so mixed up that any good qualities she possessed had been permanently tainted by lies and self-abuse.

"All right, listen up," Coach McNair announced. Jake became aware that the bus was no longer on the highway, but on a beach-front avenue. "We'll be arriving at the hotel any minute now. So that means *no* horsing around."

Jake tensed as the bus pulled in front of a large, modern-looking white stucco building. Were they here already? He glanced out the window. Yes—there was the sign, in big, bold letters: THE PARK CENTRAL. Nice place. He felt sick. He would just hop right out, check in, and go straight up to his room. No socializing. No

106

dropping in on Zoey or any of the rest of them. Straight to bed.

"All right, McRoyan; let's move it," Coach McNair said. "Unless you want to sleep in the bus."

That's not such a bad idea, Jake thought. He grabbed his bag from the rafters above the seats and followed Coach McNair.

"Hey, McRoyan—wait up," Tad Crowley called.

Jake hesitated. Tad was the last to pile out of the bus.

Tad brushed his shaggy black hair out of his eyes with a lanky arm and grinned. Jake turned to move, but Tad caught him. He waited until the rest of the kids had gone into the hotel to let Jake go.

"What's up, man?" he asked. "You feeling all right?"

Jake nodded, glancing around nervously. Even being alone with Tad Crowley for two seconds made him uncomfortable. He couldn't be with the guy and *not* think about partying.

"You look a little weird, man," Tad said.

"Yeah, well . . . I, uh, don't like flying all that much," Jake lied. "It kind of makes me sick to my stomach. The bus didn't help much."

Tad nodded thoughtfully. "Well, cheer up, McRoyan. The ride's over." He rubbed his hands together, and the corner of his lip curled up in a mischievous smile. "Another rides's about to begin."

"I don't know, man," Jake mumbled. He looked longingly at the door. Suddenly he felt very hot. "I think I might just crash tonight."

"Jake McRoyan . . . *crash?*" he mocked. He tilted his head back. "That doesn't sound right. The McRoyan I know wouldn't crash until he had taken care of some business first."

Without thinking, Jake began walking toward the

door. He just had to put as much distance as possible between himself and Tad, plain and simple. But Tad followed doggedly beside him.

"Come on, McRoyan," he whispered. "This is Miami, man. The land of ya-yo. It wouldn't be right if we didn't—"

"I don't do that anymore," Jake interrupted. He stopped and looked Tad in the eye. "Just leave me alone, all right? I can't party with you."

Tad just kept smiling, as if he thought Jake was putting on an act. "If you're freaked about the drug test, you shouldn't be. But, hey, that's cool. Screw the coke. I don't want to be up all night anyway. On the other hand, a coupla cold beers—"

"I *can't*," Jake hissed.

Tad shrugged with an exaggerated, theatrical motion. "Okay, McRoyan. Whatever you say."

"I'm serious."

"I'm sure you are," he scoffed. "Look, I'll see you in my room at around eleven . . ." His voice trailed off. He squinted over Jake's shoulders at something.

"What is it?" Jake demanded, glowering.

"My eyes must be playing tricks on me," he muttered. "I think I see some of your Chatham Island buddies."

"Oh, man . . ." Jake had been hoping to make it through just one night without having to see or talk to anybody. But sure enough, Aisha was coming across the street with some horribly sunburned blond girl he didn't recognize . . . *wait a second*. Was that *Zoey?*

Tad started to giggle. "Yo, man, didn't you used to go out with that chick?"

As much as Jake tried not to, he couldn't help but laugh along with him. Zoey looked absolutely ridiculous. Her skin was the color of a lobster shell. Her eyes met Jake's—and she froze in the middle of the street. She put her hands over her face. Aisha whispered something in her ear and yanked her along to the other side.

"Wow . . . killer tan," Tad remarked. He slapped Jake's shoulder. "I'll see you inside, man."

Jake nodded. His mouth still hung open.

"Hey, Jake!" Aisha greeted him, dragging Zoey beside her. "I was wondering if we were going to run into you. You'll have to excuse Zoey. She's feeling a little under the weather right now. . . ."

Zoey took her hands slowly away from her face. Her eyes looked like two little blue and white dots painted on to red construction paper. "Hey, Jake," she mumbled. "Nice to see you."

Jake just shook his head. A smile spread across his lips. Aisha started to chuckle. Before he knew it, all three of them were in hysterics.

"Ouch!" Zoey cried. "It hurts to laugh. . . ."

"Zoey—what *happened* to you?" he asked, once he had managed to compose himself.

"I didn't want to use sun block," she said miserably.

"Man, oh, man. I hope your face doesn't fall off."

"Thanks, Jake," she moaned. "Thanks a lot."

"So, uh, what have you guys been up to? Besides getting burned?"

"Just kind of hanging out," Zoey said. She shrugged. "We spent the whole day watching Lucas teach Kate how to surf."

"*Try* to teach Kate how to surf," Aisha put in. "I wouldn't say she's got the hang of it quite yet."

"Kate?" Jake asked. He suddenly felt a strange, nervous excitement in his stomach. He hadn't expected *her* to be with them. Not that it really mattered much, anyway. He didn't even *know* her. But she had crossed his mind more than once since that night at the Passmores' . . .

"Yeah," Zoey grumbled. She gestured across the street. "She and Lucas are still hanging out on the beach over there."

Jake strained his eyes, but he couldn't pick her out of the crowd. "Where are—"

"*McRoyan!*" Coach McNair's voice barked from behind him. "Get your butt in here!"

Jake frowned. "Duty calls," he muttered. "Look, uh, where are you guys staying?"

"Third floor," Zoey said. "Three eighteen. Are you going to have any free time? We should hang out."

Jake nodded. "Probably." Maybe it wasn't such a bad thing that he had run into them, after all. At least he hadn't seen Lara yet. He almost felt like asking, *Is Kate staying in that room, too?*—but he knew that might seem more than a little odd. It wasn't as if he could just drop in on her anyway. "I'll stop by if I get a chance," he said.

Twelve

By the time they all sat down to dinner that night in the Park Central restaurant, Zoey could hardly move. It hurt to sit. It hurt to lean back in the chair, even though it was very soft and cushiony. In fact, no matter how she positioned herself, some part of her skin would flare up with pain. She ended up sitting up straight, with her shoulders square and her back rigid.

"You know, I really don't think I'll be able to put food in my mouth," she said. She delicately placed her arms on the tablecloth and forced herself to smile. "Somebody's gonna have to feed me."

She glanced around the large, circular table. Lucas and Nina were sitting on either side of her, trying not to laugh. Aisha and Kate looked only slightly more sympathetic. Across from her, Lara, Benjamin, and Claire looked totally blank, as if their minds were on another planet.

"Did you try that Solarcaine I brought?" Kate asked. "That stuff really helps."

"Yeah, I used practically the whole bottle," Zoey mumbled. "Thanks." Kate had been nice to let her use it, so she didn't bother mentioning that the stuff didn't work. It made her feel as if she were covered in a layer of ice cold slime, but that was about it.

"I saw you run into Jake," Claire suddenly announced.

"Oh, yeah," Zoey said. She met Claire's gaze. *And thanks for opening your big mouth.* She hadn't planned on mentioning her encounter with Jake in front of Lara. Now that Lara knew he was here—in the *building*—she might go try to find him. Zoey knew that was the last thing Jake needed. "Where did you see that?" she asked.

"I was looking out my window," Claire said casually. "So what did he have to say for himself?"

"Not much." Zoey's eyes flashed to Aisha. "He's going to be really busy and he probably won't have any time to hang out at all."

"That's right," Aisha concurred, without missing a beat.

Claire shrugged. "That's too bad."

"Did he say what floor he was staying on?" Lara asked.

"No," Zoey answered firmly. "He didn't."

Kate looked around the table, confused. "Who's Jake again?"

"That's *Joke*," Nina muttered.

"He lives on Chatham Island," Zoey said. "You met him. He's got short brown hair; he's kind of big—"

"He was at my birthday party," Benjamin stated.

Zoey swallowed. The party was another subject she'd been hoping to avoid. It was obvious that Benjamin still hadn't forgiven her, even after almost two weeks. She glanced at him, but his face was unreadable behind his dark glasses.

Kate laughed good-naturedly. "No wonder I don't remember him. Hey, you know, I was actually meaning to ask you guys about something. Somebody helped me—"

"Wait a sec, Nina—I thought you liked Jake," Aisha interrupted.

"Yeah, and I also like Hootie and the Blowfish," Nina countered sarcastically. She stared at Aisha as if she'd lost her mind. "What on earth ever gave you that ridiculous idea?"

"Maybe the fact that you've been all over him the past couple of weeks," Claire cut in. A humorless little smile formed on her lips. "You wouldn't leave him alone."

Nina shot Claire a ferocious look. "I was *not* all over him. For your information—"

"All right, all right," Lucas said. He picked up a spoon and tapped it against his water glass. "That's enough. I'd like to propose a toast."

Thank you, Lucas. Zoey reached under the table and squeezed his knee. Finally somebody was doing something to end the stupid bickering.

"You're gonna toast with *water*?" Lara asked disappointedly.

Lucas ignored the question. He lifted his glass. "Here's to Kate."

Zoey's smile abruptly faded.

"I've never seen a worse surfer in my entire life," he continued, grinning broadly. "She never got up . . . but she never gave up, either. So, I say, cheers to the girl who never gives up."

Zoey took her hand away from Lucas. She couldn't believe him. Kate had made a total fool of herself this afternoon—but Lucas was praising her as if she had just won an Olympic Gold Medal.

Claire smirked. "She never *does* give up, does she? With anything."

"Claire!" Lucas barked.

Kate quickly lifted her glass. "Uh . . . I want to make

113

a toast, too. I just want to thank all you guys for letting me come with you. I know it's your senior year and everything—''

"It's not *my* senior year," Nina interrupted.

"Or mine," Lara added.

"Will you guys shut up?" Lucas demanded. "Stop interrupting her. Let her finish."

Kate put her glass down and stared awkwardly at the tablecloth. "That's okay," she said. "I'm done."

All of a sudden a wave of guilt overcame Zoey. Kate looked absolutely miserable. What was she even *feeling* right now? She had come all this way with a bunch of total strangers, only to be insulted and abused the whole time. Lucas wasn't interested in Kate; he was just trying to make her feel more at home. And Kate was just trying to make the best of a lousy situation.

"I'd like to toast Kate, too," Zoey said. She reached to lift her glass—but a burning sensation shot through her shoulder. "Ow!"

"That's quite a toast, Zo," Benjamin said dully.

Nina grabbed her glass and thrust it high into the air, spilling a few drops of water onto the table. "And *I'd* like to toast Zoey," she said in a loud, ringing voice. "Nobody wears a sunburn better. Here's to Zoey for organizing this lovely trip and motivating all of us to come down here." She waved her free hand around. "I mean, *look* at this place. Talk about swank!"

"Here, here," Kate, Aisha, and Lucas all said at once. They began knocking glasses, filling the air with a cacophonous tinkling. Zoey kept her eyes on the opposite side of the table. Claire lifted her glass, clearly somewhat reluctantly, but Benjamin and Lara remained stoic. Zoey began to get angry. Benjamin's sour mood she could understand, maybe—but what was Lara's problem? She didn't care that Lara wasn't acknowledging her with a toast; she didn't crave any attention. It was just that Lara was making a concerted effort to show everyone that she was having a bad time. She was acting like a spoiled brat.

"Sorry we don't have anything more exciting than water to toast with, Lara," Zoey said.

Lara stared at her.

Zoey felt Lucas's hand on her thigh. He was trying to soothe her, but his rubbing motion felt like hot sandpaper on her skin. "Ouch," she whispered.

He snatched his hand away. "Oops. Sorry."

Lara just shook her head. "You know what? I'm not hungry." She stood up. "Catch you guys later." She began marching out of the restaurant.

"Lara?" Benjamin called, squirming in his chair. "Lara?"

Lara disappeared into the lobby. A stunned silence fell over the table.

"Nice going, Zoey," Benjamin said after a moment.

"Shut up, Benjamin, will you?" Claire snapped. "It's Lara's fault and you know it."

"Leave him alone!" Nina cried.

Zoey put her face in her hands.

Her cheeks burned painfully, but she just couldn't bear to look at anyone right at this moment. What was happening to them?

After several seconds, she took a deep breath and looked up. Everyone at the table was staring at her.

"You know what?" she said. "I think I lost my appetite."

Lara stormed through the lobby and made a beeline for the elevators.

"Stupid little sunburned bitch," she muttered under her breath.

Leave it to Miss Holier-Than-Thou to ruin another evening. What the hell was her problem? Couldn't she understand that it was *normal* to make a toast with a real drink? But it wasn't only Zoey. *None* of them drank. It was pitiful. Every single one of those losers belonged on the *Brady Bunch.*

She pushed the elevator button agitatedly, pacing in little circles. Well, she didn't need *them* to have a good time. No—in fact, if she wanted to have a good time, she needed to forget about them completely. As soon as she got upstairs, she was going to do a little toasting of her own.

A tall, skinny boy with a baseball cap walked up and stood beside her. He punched the elevator button once, then leered at her out of the corner of his eye. She kept looking straight ahead, but she could feel his stare roving up and down her body. Her jaw tightened. She knew she shouldn't be that surprised; in her miniskirt and cut-off T-shirt, there was a lot of her body to see. But tonight she wasn't in any mood to be an object of scrutiny.

Finally she turned to look at him. "What are you looking at?" she demanded.

He grinned. He wasn't that bad-looking actually—kind of cute in a lazy, sloppy way. "Sorry," he said. "I thought I knew you. You look familiar."

She cocked an eyebrow. "That's original."

"No, seriously . . ." His eyes narrowed. "You don't happen to live in Maine, do you?"

She started to smile in spite of herself. "You've gotta be kidding me . . ."

"Do you go to Weymouth High?" he asked.

The elevator suddenly opened. "No," she said, following him through the doors. "But I know a lot of people who do."

He nodded as the elevator closed. For a moment, their eyes locked. She held his gaze. He *was* good-looking, now that she thought about it.

"Like who?" he asked, pressing for the eighth floor.

"A lot of dorks, actually," she mumbled. She reached over and pressed for the third floor.

"Sorry to hear that," he said.

"Yeah, well . . ." His baseball cap suddenly caught her eye. It had a big *W* on it. Of course: *W* for *Weymouth*. "Wait a sec—are you on the baseball team?"

He laughed. "Yeah. Why? You seen us play before?"

She shook her head. The elevator doors opened on the third floor. She hesitated.

"Hey, look," he said suddenly. "You want to come upstairs? We could play the name game for a while."

The doors started closing, but he caught them.

Her mind whirled. Yes, she wanted to go upstairs; Jake was up there. Besides, this guy was . . . *interesting*, to say the least. But she wanted to have a drink first. The problem was that Jake might not want to see her if he knew she'd been drinking. On the other hand, she could just hang out with *this* guy. . . .

"Don't worry." His lips curled up in a little half smile. "I won't bite."

"Yeah, no . . . it's uh, just that I kinda have to stop by my room first."

"Are you with your parents?"

She shook her head.

"That's cool." He shrugged noncommittally. "Listen, I'm in room eight eleven. Come on up if you feel like it. A bunch of us are just hanging out."

She nodded. "That sounds cool."

"My name's Tad, by the way," he said.

"I'm Lara."

He smiled. "Pleased to meet you, Lara."

She stepped out of the elevator and waved at him as the doors closed. "See you in a bit."

For a moment, she just stood there in the hall, processing what had happened. *That* had certainly been an odd little encounter. *Tad.* She turned the name over in her mind. The name was kind of lame—but still, he was sexy. There was something about the way he looked, about the way he presented himself, that was . . . well, a little wild. He had a glint in his eye. She always had a good instinct for people. She doubted his idea of a proper toast was the same as Zoey's.

She smiled.

After a little drink, she'd head up to room 812 and find out if her instincts were right.

Thirteen

Claire blinked a few times. Her mouth was cottony. She felt as if she could sleep for another twelve hours. She glanced at the clock. It was 10:04. She almost *had* slept for twelve hours. Nina was still fast asleep beside her, snoring lightly. She stretched, then sat up in bed.

Suddenly her eyes widened.

Lara's bed was still made.

Claire rubbed her eyes in an effort to clear the blurriness, then hopped out from under the covers. Lara's bag was lying unzipped at the foot of her bed—exactly as Claire and Nina had found it last night after dinner. Clearly, she hadn't come back to the room.

Well, well. Lara was certainly doing her best to make this vacation exciting. Claire stood for a moment, pondering the situation.

There were several possible explanations.

The first, and most likely, was that Lara had found Jake, and the two of them had spent a sordid, drunken night together.

The second was that she had been so upset after dinner that she had gone off somewhere to get drunk by herself, and subsequently passed out cold on the beach or under some barstool.

The third was that she had met a deranged serial

119

killer, who had promptly hacked her into little pieces and tossed the pieces in a dumpster.

Claire chewed the inside of her lip. She should probably tell Zoey about this. Now.

As she left the room, she saw Lucas in the hall, trying to open his door. He was in his bathing suit. His hair was wet.

"Lara's missing," she announced.

Lucas kept fiddling with the lock. "Good morning to you, Claire," he said.

"Did you just hear what I said?" she asked crossly.

Lucas nodded. "This lock is stuck. . . ."

"Lara is *missing*!" she yelled. "What is your problem?"

The lock finally clicked, and Lucas pushed the door open. "Lara's out on the beach," he said evenly. He didn't bother to look at her. "Maybe you should talk to *her* about it." The door slammed shut behind him.

Claire blinked. *On the beach.* Well, that made perfect sense. The whole point of coming down to Miami was to go to the beach, right? For a moment, she had an urge to follow Lucas into his room and scream at the top of her lungs.

A door opened behind her. Claire turned to see Zoey poking her bright red face out into the hall.

"What's going on?" Zoey asked sleepily. "I heard yelling."

"Nothing," Claire replied. "Nothing at all." She marched back into her room and immediately pulled on a pair of shorts and some flip-flops. Lucas was right. She *should* talk to Lara about it. Obviously, there had been a misunderstanding. A few ground rules needed to be established. If Lara wanted to stay out all night doing God-knows-what, fine—just as long as she told somebody that she didn't plan to go back to the room. After all, Claire could have had a whole bed to herself.

She walked determinedly to the elevators. Yes, she was going to give Lara a piece of her mind. She didn't need to waste any more time worrying about Lara McAvoy. She was going to make sure this never happened again.

By the time she reached the lobby, Claire had figured out exactly what she was going to say. She was going to start by telling Lara that under *no* circumstances could she drink in the room, and that if Claire found any alcohol . . .

Wait a second.

Claire's eyes had become drawn to two guys at the reception desk. From behind, one of them looked frighteningly like Aaron. A powerful nausea gripped her stomach. Her legs felt wobbly. Aaron even had those khakis and that exact same blue windbreaker. But he *couldn't* have come down here. The guys started to turn around. He *wouldn't* have come down. . . .

"Aaron!" she screamed.

For a moment, everyone in the lobby froze and looked at her. Then Aaron smiled and waved. He almost looked as if he'd been expecting her. The conversations around her resumed.

"What are you doing here?" she shouted, storming across the lobby. She jerked a finger toward the door. "Get the hell out of here! You hear me? Go back home! I don't have time for this!"

The smile on Aaron's face vanished. It was replaced with a look of bewildered horror. The guy next to him, obviously some boarding school dweeb by the look of his perfectly styled blonde pony tail and pressed designer jeans, was gaping at her in stunned disbelief.

"Didn't you hear me?" She stopped squarely in front

of Aaron and shoved her face into his. "*Get the hell out.*"

"Ma'am?" It was the woman behind the reception desk. Her voice was gentle but firm. "I'm going to have to ask you to keep your voice down."

"Fine." Claire lowered her voice to a harsh whisper. "Aaron—go home."

He forced a squeaky, frightened laugh. "Claire . . . uh . . . I, just flew all the way down here," he stammered. "I'm not going to just go home. . . ."

"Why not? Nobody here wants to see you."

Aaron cast a quick glance at his friend, who was still immobilized. The guy's eyes were wide. He looked scared. Claire was pleased. She wanted to inspire fear right now.

"Can we, uh, just calm down and talk for a second?" Aaron asked.

"I'm calm," she hissed. "I'm *calmly* telling you to get lost."

He tried to smile again. "But we just checked in—"

"So check out."

"I . . . I . . ."

"Why did you come here?" she asked, throwing her hands into the air. "What were you *thinking?*"

He just shook his head.

"Look, Aaron, I really don't care why you came here. Just stay out of my sight, okay?"

And with that, she turned and stormed out the door into the bright Florida morning.

Benjamin awoke to the sound of Lucas talking to himself. "I don't believe it," he was whispering. "I don't believe it." From the location of his voice, Benjamin judged that Lucas was standing in front of the window.

122

"What's going on?" Benjamin asked. Sleep still clung to his brain, making him feel as if he were talking through a fuzzy blanket. "Is something wrong?"

"Yeah, something's wrong, all right." Lucas pulled at the curtain—he was either opening or shutting it; Benjamin couldn't tell. "Aaron Mendel just walked in the front door."

Benjamin yawned. "Are you sure?"

"I just saw him. I walked over to the window, I opened the curtain, and the first thing I see is Aaron Mendel getting out of a cab."

Before Benjamin could ask any more questions, there was a knock on the door.

"Come in," Lucas called.

The door opened. "Hey, you guys." It was Zoey. "What's wrong? I heard Claire yelling in the hall a couple of minutes ago—"

"Aaron's here," Lucas interrupted.

There was a pause. "What?"

Lucas laughed bitterly. "Hard to believe, isn't it?"

"Aaron . . . ?"

"I saw him out the window. He just walked in."

Zoey didn't say anything right away. She sat on the edge of Benjamin's bed. Finally she took a deep breath. "Are you *sure?*"

"Positive," Lucas said.

Benjamin leaned against his pillow. *Oh boy*, he groaned silently. He didn't really care about Aaron one way or the other. But unfortunately, Aaron's arrival meant only one thing: a bad vacation was about to get a whole lot worse.

"Why would he come here?" Zoey asked after a moment.

"Who knows?" Lucas sighed. "Maybe he's just got a talent for showing up where he's not wanted."

"You think he's *staying* here?" Zoey asked.

"It sure looks that way."

Benjamin turned over and pulled the covers up over his head. He wished he was an inanimate object—like this mattress. He knew exactly what was going to happen now: Zoey would freak out, anticipating some imaginary crisis, and Lucas would go on and on about how he was going to kick Aaron's butt if he got a chance. Why was it that everybody he knew had to make everything so overly dramatic all the time?

"Benjamin—what's wrong?" Zoey asked.

"Nothing," he grumbled. "Look—so what if Aaron's here? It's not the end of the damn world."

Nobody said anything.

"I . . . uh, didn't say it was," Zoey mumbled after a minute.

There was another knock on the door. Nina, obviously. Benjamin frowned. "What do you want?" he yelled from under the covers.

"Is Zoey in there?" Nina asked.

"She'll be right out," he answered.

He heard Zoey start to say something, then felt the edge of the mattress spring up as she got off the bed. "No, I *won't* be right out," she breathed. She walked over to the door and opened it. "Come in."

"Uh, if this is a bad time, I can come back," Nina said in a low voice. "I just wanted to see if you guys wanted to get some breakfast—"

"Guess what?" Zoey interrupted. "Aaron Mendel's here."

Nina started laughing. "Yeah, I figured something earth-shattering had happened. I heard Claire freaking out. I thought it might have been because Lara didn't come home last night."

Benjamin pushed the covers aside and bolted upright.

"Lara didn't come home last night?" he demanded.

"Nope," Nina said nonchalantly. "Her bed was empty."

He couldn't believe his ears. Nina was acting as if losing Lara was about as serious as losing a phone number. Lara was gone—and Nina wanted to go eat *breakfast*. "What is your problem?" he shouted. "For all you know, Lara could—"

"Chill out, Benjamin," Lucas interrupted. His tone was sharp and brutal, as if he were ordering a dog to heel. "She's out on the beach. I just talked to her. You can drop the concerned parent act."

Benjamin bit his lip. He was wide awake now, quivering with a mix of emotions—frustration and embarrassment . . . but mostly anger. A lot of it was directed at himself, for acting like such a fool. But still, if it wasn't for *him*, the rest of them probably would have let Lara wander off and die somewhere by now.

"What did she say?" Nina asked.

"Not much," Lucas said flatly. "Aside from that she doesn't remember much about last night, and she's really hung over."

"Did, uh . . . she mention Jake?" Zoey asked.

"No, she didn't."

"Maybe we should talk about this somewhere else," Nina suggested quietly. "I think Benjamin wants to be left alone."

"Good idea," Lucas said. His footsteps disappeared out the room.

Benjamin sunk back into bed. Nina was right; he wanted to be left alone. Right now he wanted to be alone more than anything.

"Do you want us to bring you anything from the restaurant, Benjamin?" Nina asked.

As much as he wanted to contain his feelings, as

much as he wanted to remain perfectly relaxed, he couldn't. Nina's idiotic obsequiousness only made him more enraged. He felt as if he was struggling against a fierce tide—one with which he could no longer cope. It was much easier to just give up hope and let himself be sucked under the surface.

"Yeah," he said. "A jelly doughnut and a pair of new eyes."

Fourteen

Jake was feeling pretty good at the end of the first morning's practice. His hitting and fielding were in a lot better shape than he had expected. And the weather was perfect for baseball—cloudless and about eighty degrees. Coach McNair had even complimented him a few times. During the regular season, Coach McNair never handed out compliments—ever.

Jake had also managed to avoid talking to Tad Crowley.

Tad wasn't looking so sharp. He had struck out every time he came to the plate during batting practice, and his movement in the infield was sluggish. The bags under his eyes were a pretty clear indication of why he was having such a tough time. He'd probably been up half the night on coke and booze.

Luckily, since there were an odd number of players on the team, Jake was able to get a room to himself at the hotel. After checking in last night, he had locked the door, called Louise, and then passed out. For whatever reason, Tad hadn't come knocking. Maybe he'd gotten the picture that Jake didn't want to be involved.

"All right," Coach McRoyan called as everyone headed in from the field. "Let's move it. On the bus.

We're gonna go back to the hotel and reconvene in the lobby at two o'clock sharp. Got it?"

Jake decided to take a seat in the back this time. He was energized from the practice. If Tad Crowley had any trash talk to dish out, Jake was prepared to dish it right back.

Tad slumped down beside him. He rubbed his temples, then slowly leaned back in the seat. "You looked good out there today, Jake," he mumbled.

"Uh . . . thanks." Jake hadn't been expecting Tad to say that. He'd been expecting something along the lines of *"Where the hell were you last night, you loser?"* But he was even more taken aback by the fact that Tad had actually called him by his first name. Tad Crowley hadn't referred to him as "Jake" since freshman year.

"How are you feeling?" Jake asked tentatively.

Tad managed a feeble smile. "I'm hurting, man."

"Late night?"

"Yeah. . . ." Tad clutched his stomach as the bus jerked to a start. "Oh, man," he moaned. "It was more like an early morning. I didn't get to sleep until six."

Jake nodded. In the past, he knew he would have been envious of a statement like that. Now he only felt relief. "What happened?"

Tad glanced over at him. "I met a friend of yours."

Jake raised his eyebrows. "Oh yeah?"

"Yeah. Lara McAvoy."

A terrible, sinking feeling instantly seized him. Of course. He should have known. Lara had probably gone looking for him—and met up with Tad instead. Their meeting was inevitable. He tried to open his mouth again, but he couldn't think of anything to say.

"She's a pretty crazy girl," Tad mumbled.

Jake nodded. He looked out the window. "Tell me about it."

"She's, uh, quite a talker."

Jake whipped around. "What did she say?"

Tad chewed his lip for a moment. "You shoulda told me you were in rehab, Jake," he said quietly, so no one else on the bus could hear over the roar of the motor. "I would have understood."

Jake just shook his head. The vigorous self-confidence he'd felt all morning rapidly flowed out of him, like air out of a balloon. He could just picture the whole scenario: Lara, half naked, drunkenly waving around a bottle of tequila, ranting about how Jake McRoyan had gone to AA like a wuss, a loser, a prude . . . and Tad Crowley kicking back, eagerly egging her on in anticipation of getting laid. It was more than depressing. It was mortifying.

"I'm serious, man," Tad continued. "I had no idea. If I'd known, I would have left you alone yesterday."

Jake couldn't help but laugh at that one. "Yeah, Tad. Whatever you say."

Tad turned away. For a moment, he almost looked hurt. "You know, Jake—it's not like I would have forced you to do anything you don't want to. I just thought you were blowing me off. I wouldn't try to pull you off the wagon. I *am* your friend."

Jake had been planning on just telling Tad to shut up and mind his own business—but something in his voice made him stop. He'd never, ever heard Tad Crowley say anything like that—anything that remotely resembled an acknowledgment of friendship.

"Uh . . . what did Lara say exactly?" Jake asked.

Tad shrugged. He closed his eyes for a minute. "That you were really freaked out about drinking and that you had decided to stop."

Jake gave him a dubious look. "That's it?"

"That's about all I can remember. I was pretty

wasted." Suddenly his eyes popped open. "Hey, you aren't mad or anything? You know, that I, that *we*—"

"No." Jake shook his head adamantly. It was true. He didn't feel any sort of resentment or jealousy toward Tad whatsoever. In fact, the more he thought about it, the more he felt that Tad and Lara probably belonged together.

"You sure?"

"Yup. You know, I'm actually kind of relieved. Maybe now she'll leave me alone."

"I don't know. I doubt it, man. She wouldn't shut up about you. Even after, we, uh . . ." He didn't finish.

Jake frowned. "I thought you didn't remember."

"I *don't* remember. It was all 'Jake-this' and 'Jake-that,' on and on. I wasn't listening." He sighed. "Look, just forget it, all right? I'm sorry I brought the whole thing up. I just thought you should know."

Jake-this and *Jake-that.* Jake's stomach turned. What kind of weird things had Lara said? The night Jake had met her, she'd told him that her father was a demon. Meeting Lara McAvoy for the first time was a bizarre and scary experience. Judging from the look on Tad's face, she'd obviously said *some* strange things. It was actually pretty impressive that Tad had decided to tell Jake about the encounter. But far more impressive—or remarkable, anyway—was that he claimed to understand about Jake's drinking.

It was funny. Jake had never even considered the possibility that Tad would take "no" for an answer when it came to getting wasted. But the truth was that until this moment, he had never thought of Tad as a friend. Tad had always been a drinking partner, a teammate, a trash talker—somebody who would drink more beer and snort more lines than anyone else and then put pressure on everyone to keep up with him. Tad *was* all those things—but maybe he was changing. Or maybe he was more. Maybe in the past, Jake had just been too short-sighted to see anything else.

"Hey, man, I'm sorry," Jake suddenly said.

Tad cocked an eyebrow. "For what?"

"Uh . . . I don't know."

Tad smirked. "Well, don't worry about it. *I'm* the one who should be sorry."

The bus pulled into the drive of the Park Central and came to an abrupt halt.

"Do you think you're going to see Lara again?" Jake whispered as they filed out. "I mean, not that it's any of my business . . ."

Tad shrugged. "No idea. We didn't make plans. She wasn't there when I woke up this morning."

Jake was the last one off the bus. As soon as he stepped outside, he heard Zoey call his name.

"Jake!"

He turned to see her coming from the beach with Aisha and Nina. *And* Kate. His pulse picked up a beat.

"I'll catch you later, man," Tad said.

"Yeah," Jake said distractedly. "I'll, uh, see you this afternoon."

He fidgeted as the four of them approached. He didn't want to end this conversation with Tad just yet . . . but Kate had caught his attention. She looked very, very good. Her long red hair was wet, hanging down over her freshly tanned shoulders. And she was dressed for the beach: a bikini top, cut-off shorts, sandals—and nothing else.

"What's up, Jake?" Zoey asked.

"Oh, not much," he said. Zoey, on the other hand, wasn't looking so hot. The pants and baggy T-shirt she was wearing were obviously meant to conceal her sun-burned skin. Her nose was blistered. And she was wearing the goofiest hat Jake had ever seen—a baseball cap with the words *I'm not a tourist, I live here!* printed on the front. He grinned. "Nice hat, Zo."

"It's mine," Nina said brightly.

He rolled his eyes. "What a surprise."

"Hey Jake—you didn't happen to see Lara last night, did you?" Zoey asked suspiciously.

Jake furrowed his brow. "No. Did she say I did?"

Zoey shook her head. "She's asleep on the beach. I haven't had a chance to talk to her yet."

"Well, *I* didn't see her. She hung out with Tad Crowley all night."

"Tad Crowley?" Zoey made a distasteful face, then exchanged glances with Nina and Aisha. "Yuck. Well, *that's* interesting."

Jake didn't respond. Sometimes Zoey's unflinching belief in her own moral superiority was a little annoying. She *was* a good person—but she was also snooty. It wasn't as if Tad Crowley was Satan or anything. Neither was Lara, for that matter.

"So . . . you're the famous baseball player," Kate said with a friendly smile.

"Uh, yeah," he mumbled. Suddenly he realized he was wearing his uniform. He must have looked ridiculous. He could feel his face getting red.

She nodded. "You know, I should come by and photograph you some time."

"Uh . . . *photograph* me?"

"If you don't mind."

He shook his head, dumbfounded.

"Great. I'm doing this series on athletes for a photojournalism class. A high school baseball team would be perfect."

"Oh." His brief moment of bliss faded. She needed to take a picture of him for a college course—not because she wanted to preserve his image on film. And the way she'd said "high school baseball team" made him feel as if he should be holding a box of Cracker Jack.

"I already have some really great shots of Lucas surfing," she added enthusiastically.

He tried to smile. "That's . . . uh, great."

"Hey Jake—you'll never guess who showed up in town," Zoey said.

"Who?" He forced himself to tear his eyes from Kate.

"Aaron Mendel."

"Aaron Men—What is *he* doing here?"

"Chasing after Claire," Nina grumbled. "She ran into him this morning. He's staying at our hotel."

"Wow." Jake took a deep breath. "What did she say to him?"

"Not much," Nina said. "She pretty much just told him to drop dead, then went on her merry way."

"Has Lucas seen him yet?"

"From a distance," Zoey replied. "They haven't talked or anything."

"Yeah, well—if he gets within ten feet of him, make sure Kate's wearing a hockey mask."

Kate burst into laughter. The reaction caught Jake by surprise. He could feel himself starting to blush again. "Hey, look, you guys—I'll see you later," he said hurriedly. "The team is, uh, waiting."

"Bye, Jake," Kate called as he ran for the door.

"Bye," he called back. For some reason his voice sounded squeaky and high-pitched. Why was it that he had suddenly become a total imbecile? He could hear Nina behind him, giggling and whispering something.

One of these days, he decided, he was going to have

to make a list of people he had to wipe off the face of the earth. And Nina Geiger would be at the top of it.

Aaron paced restlessly around the hotel room. He wasn't sure how to proceed. So far, nothing had gone according to plan. But what *was* his plan? Had he really expected Claire to welcome him with open arms? He supposed he had been banking on the surprise factor: that Claire would have been so surprised to see him that she would forget all about Kate. Back in New England, that notion hadn't seemed so desperately moronic as it did now.

He should have never listened to his mother. When he had been so upset about missing Claire, she had suggested that he and George fly down to Miami and meet up with them. She had even suggested staying at the same hotel. And, like a fool, he had agreed.

"I'm bored," George announced.

Aaron glared at him. He was stretched out on the bed, staring at the ceiling. Suddenly Aaron felt as if he were in their room at school. There it seemed as if George Wallace was *always* lying on his bed, complaining about boredom. Had he come all the way to Miami to listen to this?

"Go to the beach," Aaron said.

George sat up. "Good idea. The beach will do us both some good."

"I'm gonna stay here."

George shook his head. "Aaron—you have got to forget about that chick. It's time to move on." He pointed toward the window. "Miami is *crawling* with hotties. A couple hours on the beach and I guarantee you'll forget all about what's-her-face."

"Claire," Aaron snapped. "And there's no way I'm

going to forget any time soon about what happened this morning in the lobby.''

George started laughing. ''Man . . . that *was* a pretty crazy scene, wasn't it?''

''Go ahead.'' Aaron grimaced. ''Laugh.''

''Sorry, sorry.'' George managed to contain himself. ''Look, from what I've seen, this girl is totally unbalanced. And even if she isn't, I think you should take what happened this morning as a . . . kind of divine revelation. God is telling you that you're not meant to get busy with your sister.''

''She's *not* my sis—''

''I know, I know,'' George interrupted. ''Look, man, you can sit here and sulk if you want. *I'm* gonna hit the beach.''

''Fine.''

George hopped off the bed. There was a knock on the door. He glanced at Aaron. An impish grin formed on his lips.

''Who is it?'' he asked.

''Who do you think it is?'' Claire's voice barked.

Aaron wasn't sure whether to feel relieved or terrified. For some reason, he was incapable of moving. He looked at George.

George walked to the door and opened it. ''Hi!'' he said.

Claire stood there, her arms folded across her chest, her eyes looking like two black slits.

''Can I have a minute with Aaron, please?'' she asked.

''Uh, sure . . .'' George looked over his shoulder at Aaron and winked. ''I was just leaving. By the way, I don't think we were properly introduced. My name's—''

''I'd like to talk to Aaron. Now.''

Aaron felt himself wilting. It looked as if Claire was

going to let him have it—*again*. And this time, the lady at the reception desk wouldn't be around to tell her to keep her voice down.

George chuckled. "Well . . . I guess I'll just be going." He disappeared out the door.

Claire marched in and slammed the door behind her. The noise made Aaron jump.

"Uh . . . hi, Claire," he murmured.

"I'll keep this short," Claire stated. Her voice was very calm and businesslike. She sounded as if she were about to give an oral report.

"Coming down here was a big, big mistake," she began. "I have no idea what you were thinking. You ruined my vacation—and probably everyone else's. In case you had any hopes of making up with me, I'll put them to rest. There's nothing between us. You're out of my life."

Aaron swallowed. The words had come at him so fast that he could barely comprehend their meaning. Or maybe he just didn't want to.

Claire took a deep breath. "That being said, I also want you to know that I'll forgive your mistake. I can't force you to go home. But I'm willing to put our differences aside so that we can deal with a much more important issue: our parents."

Aaron licked his dry lips. "Our parents?"

Claire nodded. "There's no *way* I'm going to let them get married."

"Uh . . . I don't think you can do much about it." In spite of his dismay and chagrin, Aaron knew that Claire didn't have a choice in the matter.

But Claire just grinned that hateful grin of hers. "I already have *done* something about it," she whispered.

"You have?" He frowned. "What?"

"That doesn't concern you," she answered briskly.

136

"I just need to know that you're behind me on this. Together, given our talents—yours at lying, mine at manipulating—I think we can pull off a breakup."

Aaron sunk down on the edge of his bed, too numb and baffled to be stung by her words anymore. Did Claire really believe she could prevent their parents from marrying? He knew Claire well enough to know that she wouldn't stop trying until failure was absolutely inevitable—or she succeeded. It was sick, in a way. Who was she to interfere in her father's life?

"Well?" she demanded.

Aaron looked at her. She *was* beautiful—mysterious and cold and alluring. But she was twisted. She was impervious to other peoples' feelings. Did he really want to have someone like her as a girlfriend, much less a stepsister for the rest of his life? At this point, he wasn't sure. Maybe Claire was right. Maybe a breakup would be best for everyone concerned.

"I'm not going to help you," Aaron said slowly. "But I won't stop you, either."

Claire regarded him with a frozen stare. "Hmmm. You promise you won't do anything to get in my way?"

He shook his head.

"Well, I guess that's good enough." She nodded, looking satisfied, then stuck out her hand. "Shake?"

He couldn't bring himself to look at her.

She seized his hand for a brief instant, then let it go. "I'll see you later," she said.

He was conscious of the door slamming, but his thoughts were still on the handshake. Part of him had been expecting—or at least hoping—to feel some kind of spark when their skin touched. But he felt nothing except shame for having succumbed to Claire's malicious whims. She was right. There was nothing between them.

Fifteen

The next few days settled into a mutually accommodating, if uneasy, routine. Zoey spent her days on the beach—smothered in level twenty-nine sun block—with Nina, Aisha, and Kate. She had given up on trying to invite Benjamin along. Thankfully so had Nina. He seemed to spend a lot of time with Lara—but mostly he preferred to stay in his hotel room, listening to music. Lara was too hungover during the day to be much of a companion, anyway. Lucas spent the days surfing by himself up the coast. And Claire lounged alone by the hotel pool.

Zoey didn't know *what* Aaron did.

At night, the seven of them would gather for a tedious and conversationless dinner—then retire to their rooms.

But by Friday afternoon, Zoey had had enough.

"You guys," she suddenly announced, after they had been broiling in post-lunch silence, "tonight we're going to do something fun. It's our last night. We've got to make it count."

"Something fun?" Nina asked, thumbing through Aisha's *Mademoiselle* for what seemed like the thousandth time. "Like what?"

"Did somebody just say something?" Aisha asked groggily. "I think I fell asleep. . . ."

"Hey—I got it!" Kate exclaimed.

Zoey sat up. "What?"

"When I went to take pictures of Jake the other day, I saw a huge ad for this bar in Coconut Grove. 'Friday Night is Teen Night. Live Reggae.' "

" 'Teen Night?' " Nina asked, sounding less than enthused.

"Yeah." Kate laughed. "Come on, you guys. I bet it's a lot of fun. You know—in a really, really cheesy way."

"That's what I'm afraid of," Nina mumbled.

"You know, you may be right," Zoey said. She smiled. "I bet they have dance contests and the limbo and stuff like that." She raised her eyebrows suggestively. "Not to mention hot guys."

Nina closed the magazine and tossed it aside. "Why would *you* care about hot guys?"

"Well, I can *look*, can't I?" she asked indignantly. "Besides—I was thinking about you all."

Aisha sighed, then rolled over on her back. "How can I appreciate a hot guy when I know that Christopher is off somewhere crawling on his belly under barbed wire? Or eating chipped beef?"

Zoey didn't even respond with so much as a glance. Aisha was seriously starting to get on her nerves. The only thing she ever did these days was complain about Christopher's absence. Zoey almost felt like telling her that if she didn't like his being gone, she should have gone ahead and married him. But then Aisha would probably start to bawl.

"Oh, yeah, Zo—I forgot to tell you," Nina said, sticking a Lucky Strike in her mouth. "I'm not interested in hot guys anymore. I've joined a radical feminist group. Our plan is to wipe out all males by the year 2000."

"I think I'm just gonna spend tonight in our room," Aisha said. "I'm gonna take advantage of the free cable. Besides, we haven't finished Nina's Twinkies yet."

Zoey shook her head. They were pathetic. If anyone should want to stay inside all night, it should be her—*she* looked like the freak, with her red and peeling skin. But no. There was nothing she could do to save the trip. It would go down in the history books as another one of Zoey Passmore's Hopeless Failures.

"Well, *I'm* psyched to go," Kate said quietly. "I'm not sure about the hot guy part, though. I think I've had my share of one-night stands."

Zoey nodded. She understood the thinly veiled reference to Aaron perfectly. A one-night stand with him would almost be enough to make somebody give up boys for good. Luckily Aaron and his friend had kept a remarkably low profile so far. She had been expecting them to be a constant nuisance. In fact, she had only seen them once since Tuesday. Maybe Aaron had finally gotten the message that he wasn't welcome among them.

"You know—I've been wondering about this now for a while," Kate said. "I mean, not to change the subject or anything, but do any of you guys know who carried me out of the house that night?"

Nina laughed. She made little quotation marks in the air. "*That night.* The night that will live in infamy."

"It wasn't Lucas?" Aisha asked.

"I don't know. I don't think so."

Zoey thought for a minute. She thought she had remembered it being Jake, but she wasn't sure. Everything had happened so fast. "Why do you want to know?" she asked.

"Oh, I don't know." Kate had a faraway look in her

eyes. "I guess it doesn't matter. I'm just kind of curious."

Zoey shrugged. "Well, if you ask me, I think we should forget about that night. You made it out alive, and that's the important thing."

"Hey, Zoey?" Nina said. "Do you honestly think Benjamin will be willing to go to something called 'Teen Night'?"

Aisha laughed. "Yeah—he *did* just turn twenty, after all. 'Teen Night' is way beneath him."

"Probably not," Zoey admitted. "But I don't think that should stop us. Unless we want to go to a three-hour opera, Benjamin's not going to be psyched on anything we suggest."

Nina picked up the magazine again. "Well, I just don't think we should leave him out," she said.

Zoey shrugged. "You feel like going to a three-hour opera?"

"You know what?" Aisha said. "I think I actually could be psyched for reggae night. I love reggae."

Nina snorted. "Eesh—you do *not* love reggae. You don't know the first thing about it."

"How do you know?" Aisha tried to sound offended, but she ended up smiling.

Nina looked meaningfully at her over the edge of the magazine. "Because your musical taste bites. Name one Bob Marley song."

"Well, I can't think of any *songs*. . . ." She paused. "But I always like reggae when I hear it," she added uncertainly.

Nina turned back to the magazine. "Spoken like a true connoisseur," she scoffed.

"Okay, I'm sorry I don't like music that sounds like machine-gun fire, but—"

"Then it's settled," Zoey interrupted. She was in no

mood for a lame argument over taste in music. "Aisha—you're coming."

Aisha sighed. "Yeah. Now that I think about it, cable TV and Twinkies might be just a tad too depressing for our last night of vacation."

Nina put the magazine down again. "Well, now I'm gonna *have* to go. I mean, we are the four musketeers, aren't we?"

Zoey almost laughed, but the situation was too grim. She could see now what would happen: Claire and Benjamin would refuse to go; Jake would be too tired; and Lucas would mope about being the only guy. Nina was right. They *were* the four musketeers—but only by default. She stuck her hand into the air. "All for one and one for all," she said lethargically.

Kate sat up and looked toward the road. "Hey—here comes Jake."

Zoey turned around. He waved as he walked across the beach, then sat down beside them.

"What's up?" Zoey said.

"Not much." For some reason, he seemed nervous. "Coach McNair gave us the afternoon and the night off." He spoke quickly and looked at the sand. "We have an eleven o'clock curfew—but we're free until then."

Kate smiled. "Curfew. That reminds me of boarding school."

"Boarding school was probably a lot more fun than baseball camp," he mumbled.

"Well, *I* know something fun you can do," she said.

He looked up. "Uh . . . what's that?" he asked uncertainly.

"You can come with us to this club in Coconut Grove. Tonight is 'Teen Night.' "

Jake grinned. "Yeah—I saw that sign, too. The Baja Beach Club, right?"

Kate nodded. "You in?"

"Sure."

Zoey peered at Jake closely. She hadn't been expecting him to agree so quickly. If *she* had suggested it, he probably would have said no. But he was staring at Kate in the same way that Lucas always did—as if she were some kind of goddess. Zoey frowned.

Nina took a long drag on her Lucky Strike. "Hey, Jake—what's up with Lara and Tad Crowley?"

Jake shrugged. "I have no idea. I've seen her in the hall a couple of times—but Tad hasn't mentioned anything more about it."

"But Lara's left you alone?" Zoey asked.

"So far."

"Wait a sec," Kate said in a teasing, half-serious voice. "Does Lara have a crush on you or something?"

Suddenly Jake leapt up. "I think I'm gonna go for a swim," he muttered. He dropped his towel and bolted for the water.

Kate glanced at Zoey. "Whoops," she whispered. "I didn't mean to embarrass him or anything. . . ."

"Oh, don't worry about it," Zoey said. Secretly, she couldn't help but be relieved that Kate Levin, the perfect woman, had finally put her foot in her mouth. She *was* fallible, despite what every male on the planet seemed to believe. "Jake's just in a bad mood these days because he and Lara used to go out. Lara's having a harder time with the breakup than he is."

Kate nodded, as if she were looking for Zoey to continue. But that was enough information, Zoey decided. Kate didn't need to know the rest of the sordid details.

"Well, I didn't mean to make him feel bad," she said

143

finally, watching Jake as he bobbed around in the waves.

"I wouldn't worry about it, Kate," Nina said. She grinned slyly at Zoey. "Jake's not the type to hold a grudge." She stood up and brushed the sand off her T-shirt. "Speaking of grudges and hard breakups, I think I'm going to take a shot at seeing if Benjamin wants to come with us tonight. I'll see you guys in a bit."

"You sure?" Aisha asked, looking at Zoey.

"Yeah," Nina said. She lowered her eyes and began walking away. "Who knows? Maybe he'll be psyched."

Zoey could tell from Aisha's expression that they were thinking the same thing: *Maybe he won't.* Benjamin had spent the entire vacation blowing Nina off in the harshest and most blatant possible way. And as much as Zoey hoped that Nina's perseverance would pay off—she was beginning to have her doubts. She was beginning to wonder if the Benjamin Passmore of old was gone forever.

"Good luck," Zoey called after her.

"Thanks," Nina answered. She didn't look back. "I'm gonna need it."

BENJAMIN

I've given up on friendship. I guess it's
just not that important to me. Not that I
ever put much stake in it, anyway.
Having a lot of friends has never been a
big priority in my life. I've always been
too busy worrying about other things—
like finding the bathroom, or making it
across the street without tripping and
falling flat on my face.

As I see it, maintaining friendship is
pretty much a waste of time. People are
unreliable. Just when you think that
somebody respects you, you realize that
they pity you instead. It makes me
angry, but there isn't a whole lot I can
do about it. It's hard not to seem pitiful
when you're blind.

Blindness, blindness, blindness. That's
all anyone can think about when they're
around me. Maybe blind people
shouldn't have sighted friends. I've
actually been thinking about this quite a
bit recently. I think I would probably get
along a lot better with someone who
understands where I'm coming from—
someone who shares my anger and my
frustration. Sighted people just don't
get it.

Another problem with sighted people is that most of them are stupid.

Whoops. I seem to have forgotten about the question. How would I define friendship? Well, for one thing, it's knowing when to keep quiet and leave someone alone. I guess it's also knowing how to make someone laugh. No wonder I've given up on friendship. Nobody can make me laugh. Then again, the only people I know are sighted.

Sixteen

Benjamin could barely hear the pounding on the door over Tito Puente's drumming. He had deliberately turned up the radio in order to drown out any other noise. For a second, he was tempted to ignore whoever it was. But he couldn't exactly pretend he wasn't here. He sighed, then got up off the bed and turned down the music.

"Who is it?" he asked.

"Nina," came the reply.

He shook his head. Was it that difficult to understand that he wanted to be left alone? "What is it, Nina?" he asked.

"Can, uh . . . I come in?"

"Fine." He stormed across the room and fumbled for the doorknob, then threw open the door. "What do you want?"

She quickly ducked past him. "I was knocking, for like, five minutes," she mumbled. "Don't you think you might be hurting your ears?"

He closed the door—*hard*—then walked back over to the radio. "I like it loud." He turned up the volume again.

"I guess so," she shouted. "Well, if you like loud music, you're gonna love what I have in store for you."

"What's that?" he yelled, lying back down on the bed.

The music suddenly faded.

"Do you mind if I turn it down?" she asked.

He sat up. "Actually, I do."

"This won't take very long. I promise."

"Fine." His head flopped back down on the pillow. "What is it?"

"We're going to hear live reggae tonight."

"Have fun. Now can you please turn the music back up?"

For a few moments, the room was quiet. "Come on, Benjamin," Nina said softly. "It'll be fun. Besides—I thought you liked Caribbean music. That's what you're listening to, right?"

"I was listening to *jazz*, Nina," he spat. "Latin Jazz. It has absolutely nothing to do with reggae, other than it comes from the same hemisphere."

She took a deep breath. "Well, excuse me." Her voice was quavering a little. "Not all of us are as musically enlightened as you."

He ran his hands through his hair. He felt bad about snapping at her—but there was no way he would go hear some corny reggae band with the whole Chatham Island crew. "Look, Nina," he said. "I, uh, just don't like reggae all that much. To tell you the truth, I was just planning on staying here and listening to the radio all night. The stations in Miami are amazing. I want to listen to them as much as possible before I leave."

"Come on, Benjamin," she protested. "That's ridiculous. You'd rather listen to the *radio* than hear live music? You can buy all that stuff on CD, anyway."

He forced himself to remain even-tempered. "The answer's no, Nina," he said simply.

Nina sat down on the bed beside him. "But I hear

this band is amazing. They're advertised as the Boston Philharmonic of reggae. I'm not making that up. 'Even reggae haters like Benjamin Passmore will love the smooth sounds of this unique reggae outfit.' That's what the sign said. I swear.''

He groaned. "Very funny. I'm not going, Nina. I'm sorry. You guys have fun."

"Well, to be honest with you, I don't like reggae myself all that much," she said. He could feel the weight of the mattress shift as she stretched out beside him. "As a matter of fact, I could be psyched to listen to the radio, too. As long as we listen to Rush Limbaugh."

"Nina—what are you doing?" he asked. He inched away from her.

"What do you mean?"

"Why are you lying down next to me?"

"I'm tired." She laughed once. "Jeez, Benjamin—I won't *touch* you. Anyway, these beds are big enough for an entire football team. And we both know that cooties can only be transmitted through direct physical contact. Or by passing notes in class."

Benjamin suddenly realized he was grinding his teeth. He was furious. There was no humor in this situation— none at all. Nina's lame jokes were only making him angrier. "I want to be alone, all right?" he shouted. "Can't you get that through your thick skull?"

"Well, can't you get it through *your* thick skull that I don't *want* to leave you alone?" she shouted back. "Can't you understand that all of us are worried sick about you?"

For a moment, the room was dead quiet. Benjamin held his breath. He didn't want to hear this right now; he didn't *need* to hear this. Finally he let the air out of his lungs.

"There's nothing to worry about," he said in a hollow voice. "You can tell all of them that. Tell them that I'm fine—but I just want to be alone." He rolled over so that his back was to her. "I've got a good idea. Why don't you go tell them right now?"

Nina didn't answer. His ears perked up. He realized that she was crying softly.

"Why are you making this so hard on yourself, Nina?" he whispered. "What do you want me to say?"

"I want you to say that you're going to start acting like yourself again," she sobbed.

He curled up into a ball on the mattress. He hated to witness her lose control like this, but there was nothing he could do about it. "This is myself," he said.

"No, it's not." She sniffed. "It's some other person. It's some other person who has nothing to do with Benjamin Passmore."

"That doesn't make any sense, Nina. I'm *me*. This is who I am. If you don't like it . . ."

"Then how come everybody else feels the same way I do?" she cried. "How come everybody else feels as if they don't know you anymore?"

"Maybe they don't," he said quietly. "Maybe I've changed."

"But I love you, Benjamin." Her voice was pleading. She put a trembling hand on his back. "I love you so much."

He twisted away and pushed himself off the bed. This conversation had gone on long enough. It was too painful. He had to tell her in no uncertain terms what he felt.

"Nina," he said. "I don't love *you*."

She didn't try to argue. He heard her jump off the bed, then felt the breeze as she rushed past him, disappearing out the door and down the hall—and then her footsteps faded into silence.

150

Seventeen

As soon as she walked through the doors of the Baja Beach Club, Claire swore to herself that she would never let Zoey talk her into anything like this again. Even hanging out in the hotel room and listening to Nina blubber all night would have been preferable to *this*. She had never seen a sadder-looking bunch of oafs assembled in one place at one time. Every single boy— without exception—was wearing a baseball cap. Every single girl was sunburned and caked with makeup. And the room was packed. She could hardly move.

". . . up to the front?" Zoey was yelling.

"What?" Claire yelled back. Bass and drums were pumping at her from every direction. Her spine vibrated with each beat.

Zoey stuck her face next to Claire's ear. "The band's up front. You wanna go up there?"

"No, thanks." Claire glanced at Jake, Lucas, and Aisha. They all looked as horrified as she felt. Only Kate seemed to be enjoying herself. She had a huge smile on her face. Her body was swaying in time to the music.

"I told you this was gonna be cheesy!" Kate cried. "Come on!" She grabbed Zoey's hand and yanked her forward. The two of them instantly vanished into the mob.

"Great." Lucas shook his head angrily. "What the hell am I supposed to do now?"

Jake stood on his tiptoes, desperately trying to follow them. "Come on, man," he said. "I think I see them. . . ."

A moment later, the two of them disappeared as well.

Claire looked at Aisha. "What do you think?" she yelled.

Aisha raised her eyebrows. "I think we should get into a cab and go back to the hotel," she yelled back.

Claire smirked. That wasn't such a bad idea, actually. She was still a little worried about Nina, even though Nina had insisted that everything was fine and that she just wanted to be alone. She refused to tell anyone what Benjamin had said this afternoon. Whatever it was, it was serious. Claire knew all too well how cold Benjamin could be. She just hoped he hadn't mentioned their kiss, for Nina's sake. It had been almost two weeks. And it had been pretty insignificant, anyway—a curious fluke more than a moment of real passion.

"You know, I think I'm going to go up front for a bit," Aisha said, scanning the crowd. "I paid five bucks. I might as well try to get my money's worth."

Claire nodded. "Suit yourself. I think I'll wait outside."

She watched as Aisha was swallowed up by the swarm. Then she turned and pushed her way outside. If she ever came back to Miami, she would have to remember never to set foot again in the Baja Beach Club.

The parking lot was a cool, quiet relief from the sweaty raucous club. Claire sat down on a bench and closed her eyes for a second. Solitude was what she craved. She envisioned what it was like on her widow's walk right now—cold and windy. She couldn't wait to get back there. She couldn't wait to have some real time by herself. . . .

The letter. She had forgotten all about it in the past few days. It had probably gotten there by now. Her heartbeat increased. Maybe the midget would be gone by the time she got home.

"Claire!" a raspy, unfamiliar female voice shrieked.

Claire opened her eyes to see three figures stumbling across the parking lot toward her—a girl and two boys. She strained her eyes.

All at once she gasped.

It was Lara—with Aaron and his friend.

"Claire!" Lara yelled again. For some reason, her voice didn't sound like her own. She laughed. She was weaving, lilting from side to side. "Look who I foun'."

The three of them stopped in front of the bench. Claire's face shriveled in revulsion. The smell of alcohol was powerful, even from several feet away.

"Aaron's here!" Lara cried, throwing her arms around his neck. "Isn' that great?"

Aaron grinned. He was barely able to stand. His hair was mussed. He looked appalling.

"So I see," Claire murmured.

"Hi, Claire!" Aaron's friend said, a little too loudly.

Claire ignored him. She stared at Lara. "How did you three hook up?" she asked.

"I foun' . . . I foun' 'em in the lobby," Lara stammered. "Aaron and George here asked me if I wanted to get a drink." She threw her hands up and cackled. "It was an offer I couldn't refuse!"

"Well." Claire's eyes flashed to Aaron. "I have to hand it to you, Aaron—you always make the best of a bad situation."

He pitched forward slightly. "Wassat supposed to mean?" he slurred.

"Well, you already ruined your chances with Zoey, Kate, and me . . . so you went for the easy target."

"Easy?" Lara demanded. Her smile was gone. "How would *you* know, you stuck-up bitch?"

"Okay, okay," Aaron said, putting his finger over his mouth. "Shhhh . . ."

Claire shook her head gently. "It's fine." Lara's behavior was far too pitiable to warrant any anger. "I'm sorry, Lara; that was unfair. You're not easy. By the way, where's Tad?"

"By the way, where's Tad?" Lara imitated in a piercing, nasal voice. "For your information, *Claire*, I don't give a crap. That kid's a loser."

"Oh? I thought you two got along."

Aaron's friend lurched toward the entrance. "This conversation's boring," he said. "I'll see you in there."

"Wait up!" Lara called, chasing after him. "I'm comin' with you. I gotta find Jakie. I gotta talk to Jakie. . . ."

Claire shook her head as the two of them staggered into the club. Poor Jake. How he had ever let himself get involved with that freak was still a total mystery to her.

"Wassup, Claire?" Aaron asked, sitting down beside her.

Claire slid as far away as possible from him on the bench. "Come on," he said, making a sad little puppy dog face. "Truce?"

"You better go inside," she said blandly. "Lara might get lonely."

"Nah . . ."

"It's not a suggestion, Aaron."

Aaron just laughed. He moved a little closer to her, breathing whatever kind of liquor they'd been drinking into her face. She wanted to vomit.

"Back off," she warned.

"Don't worry, Claire. I'm not gonna try anything. If you wanna know the truth, you make me sick."

The muscles in the back of Claire's neck tensed. Rage was starting to boil inside her. "I'm glad," she hissed. "The feeling's mutual."

"Hey, Claire . . . is the reason you're so frigid because you're a virgin?"

She slapped him.

"Whoa!" he cried—but he was laughing.

"Stay the hell away from me!" she shouted.

"Claire . . ."

She ran across the parking lot. She didn't know or care where she was going; she just needed to get away from him. Before she even knew it, she was sprinting as fast as she could, fueled by hatred and anger—but by something else as well: shame.

The secret's out, she realized.

How had he found out? Had he guessed? Had he known by the way she'd been talking about that party so much that she must have been expecting to lose her virginity?

She could still hear that derisive, drunken laughter.

It's only a matter of time before everyone else finds out the truth, too.

There was nothing she could do about it now. All that was left to her was retribution. But she was going to make him pay for what he said. She would make him pay for chasing her down here. She would make him pay dearly.

Jake stood against the wall by the side of the stage, watching hopelessly as Aisha, Zoey, and Kate danced in the crowd, encircled by a ring of hungry-looking boys. He wanted to get in there and dance with Kate

. . . but he knew he'd just end up making a fool of himself. He was a lousy dancer and he knew it. Besides, the sad truth was that Kate only seemed to think of him as a "high school baseball player"—in other words, a cute little boy, and one she would never consider in any kind of romantic way.

He glanced over at Lucas, standing beside him. Lucas looked even more upset than he did. In fact, he looked angry. His eyes were fixed to the three or four guys who were staring very intently at his girlfriend.

"*Ja-kee . . .*"

Jake's ears perked up. He scanned the crowd. He could have sworn he heard someone calling his name.

"*Ja-kee . . .*"

Oh, no. He knew that voice.

"Jak-ee!"

The voice was right in front of him. Then he saw her. Lara squeezed herself between a couple dancing, then toppled into him.

"There you are!" she cried.

Jake winced and drew his head back, trying to escape the stench of tequila. He pulled her roughly to her feet. "Lara—"

"I'm *sooo* glad to see you," she said, putting her hands on his chest. "Haven't I been a good girl?"

She was wearing a tiny T-shirt that revealed her belly button and very tight jeans, but Jake felt no attraction whatsoever. He shook his head, totally repulsed. "You're not making any sense."

"C'mon." She began digging her fingernails into his shirt. "I left you alone all week—"

He grabbed her hand. "Don't *touch* me," he said. Lucas had turned to look at him—but thankfully none of the others had noticed yet.

"But don' you unnerstan'?" She belched, then

slapped a hand over her mouth. "Oops. 'Scuse me. Don't you get it? I left you alone 'cause I knew you had practice."

Jake laughed. Did she really think he would believe that? She must have been really, really bombed. "Lara—you left me alone because you were with Tad Crowley."

He felt a hand on his shoulder. It was Lucas. "I'll catch you later, man," he said. "Looks like you got your hands full." He headed in the direction of the door.

Lara grabbed his chin, forcing him to look her in the eye. "I only . . . I only did that to make you mad," she whispered hoarsely, but loud enough to be heard over the music.

"Well, it didn't work," Jake said in a flat voice. "It didn't work one bit."

"But I don't *like* Tad," she whined.

"Too bad for him," he mumbled.

"Ja-kee! I like *you*."

"Lara—go away, all right? It's over. We aren't a couple anymore, okay? I don't even know if we're friends."

She shook her head rapidly. "I don' believe it," she said. She stuck her hands out, as if she had suddenly lost her balance. Then she grinned at him. "Unless there's somebody else . . ."

Jake looked over Lara's shoulder. He could see Kate now, in her black miniskirt, dancing with her head down and her red hair flailing wildly over her shoulders to the monotonous, steady beat of the reggae band. Until he had seen her, he had thought he was going to tell Lara no.

"Yes," he said. "There is. Only she doesn't know it."

"I don't believe you, Jakie."

Jake looked her in the eye. "Believe it." He pushed her away, then lost himself in the crowd.

*   *   *

Lucas struggled to shove his way toward the exit, but the wall of people was too dense. All of a sudden he heard a loud cheer erupt from the entrance. The crowd in front of him bulged. He shook his head. It was useless to try to move.

"Lucas?" Zoey's voice yelled in his ear.

He turned around. She was standing next to him, but she was losing her footing. "What's wrong?" she asked.

"I've gotta get out of here," he said. "It's too crowded."

She reached out and grabbed his hand. "I'll come with you."

He smiled. Finally—after all this time—she was agreeing to do something *he* wanted to do. He turned around and forced his way through the onslaught of people, ignoring the pushing and the angry comments. Soon he became aware of something: everyone in front of him was wearing a green uniform. He frowned. He was surrounded by *soldiers*. At least—they looked like soldiers, even though they weren't carrying guns or anything. What was going on here? Wasn't this supposed to be 'Teen Night'?

"Keep going," Zoey shouted.

He lowered his head and barreled through the last mass of people. At last he saw the door. He lunged the final few feet, dragging Zoey out behind him.

"Whew!" he said breathlessly. "Man. It's a good thing we got out when we did."

Zoey nodded, staring confusedly at the steady stream of soldiers filing through the entrance. "I wonder what this is . . . ?"

"Who cares?" Lucas seized her arm and pulled her into the parking lot. "All I know is, we would have suffocated if we stayed in there any longer."

"That *was* pretty crazy," she admitted. She pointed to a bench. "You want to sit down?"

"Yeah." He hadn't even realized how badly his legs were aching until he felt the relief of easing down on the bench. "Man . . . that feels good."

Zoey ran a hand through his hair.

"*That* feels pretty good, too," he added, closing his eyes and basking in the sensation.

"Are you having fun?" she asked.

"Now I am," he whispered. "I was waiting . . ."

She took her hand away. "Hmmm. Isn't that Claire over there?"

Lucas opened his eyes. He squinted in the direction of Zoey's finger. A girl who very well may have been Claire was sitting alone at the edge of the parking lot, her face buried in her hands. Lucas sighed. "So?"

"Maybe I should go over and see what's wrong. . . ."

Lucas put a hand on her knee. "Nothing's wrong, Zo," he said. "She probably just wants to be left alone. That's what she always wants."

Zoey bit a fingernail. "I don't know. . . ."

"Fine," he snapped, taking his hand away. He knew there was no legitimate reason to be mad, but he just couldn't control himself. He hadn't had a single moment alone with her this entire vacation. She always had to be checking up on people, making sure they were okay. She needed to learn how to mind her own business.

"What's wrong?" she asked.

"Nothing. It's just that you never seem to wonder if anything's wrong with *me*."

She shook her head, looking bewildered. "Is there?"

"What's wrong is that you've been ignoring me ever since we got here."

"I, I—" she stammered. "I've been ignoring *you!* You're the one who's gone surfing every day. And the rest of the time . . ." She broke off.

"What?"

She avoided his eyes. "The rest of the time you've been totally focused on Kate."

"Zoey—she's my *guest!* Of course I'm focused on her. She's been having a terrible time. I mean, Claire's been totally at her throat, and then Aaron showed up—"

"How would you know?" Zoey interrupted.

He paused, caught off guard by the question. "What do you mean?"

"You haven't spent any time at all with Kate, Lucas. You surf all day. *I'm* the one who's been making sure that she has a good time. *I'm* the one who's spent every single minute of my vacation with *your* houseguest."

Lucas laughed. "Listen to what you're saying, Zoey. You just contradicted yourself. You said I'm focused on Kate, and then you turn around and say I'm not spending any time with her."

Zoey opened her mouth, then snapped it shut. Her eyes narrowed. "Fine, Lucas. You're right. Well, I'm going to go back inside and make sure that *your* houseguest is enjoying herself. I'll catch you later."

Lucas stared at her, totally speechless, as she marched back into the club. He couldn't believe what had happened to them. They were the only two people on this entire trip who were remotely sane. But it didn't seem as if they were going to get along again—ever. Maybe that quiz was right. Maybe they were a "lost cause."

"Zoey?" he called.

But she was already gone.

Aisha felt herself being pushed farther and farther toward the stage. Suddenly she realized she had lost *both* Zoey and Kate. She looked around, slightly pan-icked. She had to make a break for it—now.

For some reason, everyone around her seemed to be wearing some kind of military uniform. *And* they were all men. They were all staring at her. This wasn't good. She bent her head and began squirming through the throng. There were a few comments: "Where ya goin', sugar?" and "Stick around, babe!" No wonder Zoey and Kate had left. She was surrounded by a troop of male chauvinist pigs.

As she neared the entrance, she finally found herself with a little more space to breathe. She shook her head. Were the guys in Christopher's outfit like these guys? She hoped not. He tended not to cope very well with meatheads.

She took a few quick steps toward the door—and stopped dead in her tracks.

Christopher was standing there, in one of those stupid green polyester uniforms, not five feet in front of her.

No, she said to herself. It couldn't be true. The heat and lack of oxygen must have been playing tricks on her mind. Obviously: she had just been *thinking* about him, so naturally she would imagine *seeing* him. . . .

"Aisha?" he asked. He blinked several times. His mouth fell open. "Oh my God—*Aisha*?"

She swallowed. Her feet seemed to move toward him of their own volition. Her eyes kept roving over his trim, muscular frame, unconsciously seeking a reason to doubt that Christopher Shupe was really standing *here*. In the flesh. At the Baja Beach Club. On Teen Night.

He broke into a rapturous smile. "It *is* you. . . ."

Before she knew it, he had taken her in his arms and was squeezing her as tightly as he possibly could. Tears began streaming down her face. She still thought she must have been dreaming. It just didn't make any sense.

Finally they stepped apart.

"What are you *doing* here?" they both asked simultaneously.

Aisha laughed, brushing the tears away from her face. "You first," she said.

"We're on leave," he said. His eyes were still wide. "There was a transport plane flying down to Miami, so I thought I'd hitch a ride. . . ." He shook his head. "Man. This is so crazy."

She took his hand. "I heard you called."

He nodded. "Yeah. I was gonna tell you that I had leave. Your mom said that you were really busy. Some test or something. . . ."

For the briefest instant, a vision of David Barnes flashed through her mind, but the next moment it was gone. She drew Christopher close. "I've been thinking about you so much," she whispered.

He lifted his eyebrow in that cocky, half-serious way he had—that look that had intoxicated her from the moment she'd first laid eyes on him. "Probably not as much as I've been thinking about you," he murmured.

She couldn't stop crying. "I can't believe it's really you," she wept, burying her face in his shoulder.

"It is, baby," he breathed. He gently stroked her hair. "It's me."

"How long are you here for?" she asked.

"Just tonight."

She took a deep breath and looked him in the eye. "Can you spend it with me?" she asked.

He kissed her. The sensation filled her with a joy she hadn't believed was possible to feel since the night he had proposed.

"Of course I can, Eesh. Of course I can."

Making Out:
Lara Gets Even

Book 16 in the explosive series about broken hearts, secrets, friendship, and of course, love.

Lara loves **Jake** but so does **Kate**——only she doesn't know it yet. **Jake's** fallen for **Kate,** and unless **Lara** can persuade **Kate** that **Ben's** the one she really wants, **Lara** will lose **Jake** forever. Too many people have too much to lose when…

Lara gets even

A fantasy, a love story, a summer of change...

The China Garden

By LIZ BERRY

AVON
tempest

"Like a jewel box with hidden drawers and
compartments, this finely crafted, multilayered
novel holds many secrets...richly laden with
mystery and suspense, in which the ordinary
often masks unexpected interconnections
and the extraordinary is natural to the story's
wildly imagined terrain."
—PUBLISHERS WEEKLY ☆

Love stories just a little more perfect than real life...

Don't miss any in the

enchanted ♥ HEARTS

series:

ehs 0499

READ ONE...READ THEM ALL—
The Hot New Series about Falling in Love

M A K I N G   O U T

by KATHERINE APPLEGATE

(#1) Zoey fools around	80211-2 /$3.99 US/$5.50 Can
(#2) Jake finds out	80212-0/$3.99 US/$4.99 Can
(#3) Nina won't tell	80213-9/$3.99 US/$4.99 Can
(#4) Ben's in love	80214-7/$3.99 US/$4.99 Can
(#5) Claire gets caught	80215-5/$3.99 US/$5.50 Can
(#6) What Zoey saw	80216-3/$3.99 US/$4.99 Can
(#7) Lucas gets hurt	80217-1 /$3.99 US/$4.99 Can
(#8) Aisha goes wild	80219-8/$3.99 US/$4.99 Can
(#9) Zoey plays games	80742-4/$3.99 US/$4.99 Can
(#10) Nina shapes up	80743-2/$3.99 US/$5.50 Can
(#11) Ben takes a chance	80867-6/$3.99 US/$5.50 Can
(#12) Claire can't lose	80868-4/$3.99 US/$5.50 Can
(#13) Don't tell Zoey	80869-2/$3.99 US/$5.50 Can
(#14) Aaron lets go	80870-6/$3.99 US/$5.50 Can